High Tide

Armand Rosamilia, Tom Duffy

Rymfire Books

Copyright © 2025 by Armand Rosamilia, Tom Duffy

All rights reserved.

No portion of this book may be reproduced in any form without written permission from the publisher or author, except as permitted by U.S. copyright law.

Armand's Mailing list

Are you a fan of suspense thrillers?

Join Armand Rosamilia's mailing list
Lots of exclusive content, news about upcoming thriller books,
appearances and more.
Sign up now and get a free story, too!
https://armandrosamilia.com

Contents

1. ONE   1
2. TWO   6
3. THREE   12
4. FOUR   18
5. FIVE   23
6. SIX   28
7. SEVEN   33
8. EIGHT   39
9. NINE   44
10. TEN   49
11. ELEVEN   54
12. TWELVE   59
13. THIRTEEN   64
14. FOURTEEN   69
15. FIFTEEN   74
16. SIXTEEN   79

17.	SEVENTEEN	84
18.	EIGHTEEN	89
19.	NINETEEN	94
20.	TWENTY	100
21.	TWENTY-ONE	105
22.	TWENTY-TWO	110
23.	TWENTY-THREE	115
24.	TWENTY-FOUR	120
25.	TWENTY-FIVE	125
26.	TWENTY-SIX	130
27.	TWENTY-SEVEN	135
28.	TWENTY-EIGHT	140
29.	TWENTY-NINE	145
30.	THIRTY	150
31.	THIRTY-ONE	155
32.	THIRTY-TWO	160
33.	THIRTY-THREE	165
34.	THIRTY-FOUR	170
35.	THIRTY-FIVE	175
36.	THIRTY-SIX	180
37.	THIRTY-SEVEN	185
38.	THIRTY-EIGHT	190

39.	THIRTY-NINE	195
40.	FORTY	200
41.	FORTY-ONE	205
42.	FORTY-TWO	210
43.	FORTY-THREE	215
44.	FORTY-FOUR	220
45.	FORTY-FIVE	225
46.	FORTY-SIX	230
47.	FORTY-SEVEN	236
48.	FORTY-EIGHT	241
49.	FORTY-NINE	246
50.	FIFTY	251
About the Author		257
About the Author		258

ONE

"Do you know what bothers me, Enrique, more than anything? A whiner." Diego Santiago sighed. "I need you to say words, actual words that form sentences. Words that tell me what you know and don't know, and then I can get you to hospital. With any luck you'll survive."

Diego scooped up the bloody fingers off of the table and sighed again. "I mean, let's be honest... they won't be able to sew these back on your hand, but at this point I haven't taken the other fingers off the other hand."

Enrique, his hand a bloody stump and his teeth spread across the floor of the warehouse, was in and out of consciousness. He was whispering something over and over, but Diego couldn't understand what the man was saying.

Diego didn't want to get too close to Enrique and get his suit dirty, either.

"I need him to answer the questions and tell me what I want to know," Diego said to the three men in the room with them, all torturers he could count on. Normally, Diego would have one or maybe two doing the work, but he needed to know about the missing plane that Enrique had seen off of the coast six months ago.

A plane that was not only filled with cartel cocaine and meth but also six old chests supposedly filled with treasures that had been taken from an old Aztec pyramid from the deep jungle.

It was a treasure Diego knew a lot of people were looking for, and Enrique had watched as the plane slammed into the Pacific Ocean off the coast. As a local spotter, his job was to immediately let the cartel know the plane had gone down and where it was.

Instead, Enrique had tried to take the drugs and sell them on his own, and get out of the country.

Lucky for the cartel, Enrique had gone to a corrupt DEA agent to sell the coke and meth.

Diego didn't care about the coke and meth, though. That was a drop in the bucket. The cartel saw it as an acceptable loss, and they would make more and more or import it in for resale.

No, the six chests were what was important to Diego right now. The fact he'd only just learned about the chests was upsetting to him, and he'd made sure Enrique knew how upset it had made him.

Enrique had never mentioned the chests, but it stood to reason he'd managed to take everything from the plane. Where was he hiding it all, though? Six wooden chests were heavy, especially if they were loaded with Aztec gold. A couple of cigarette boats could be used to load and unload the drugs, but it might take more than that for the rest.

"Where are the chests?" Diego yelled at Enrique, who'd passed out again.

Diego sighed yet again. He needed answers and soon. Before anyone else in the cartel or any of their many enemies heard about the treasure and started to look for it themselves.

"I want an answer from him, before you kill him. Do you understand? This is important and there is a nice bonus in this for all of you," Diego said. "I will be getting lunch. Call me when you have my answer."

Diego walked out of the warehouse and right into the back of his black SUV, telling the driver to crank the air conditioning. He didn't like getting his hands dirty and sweating, yet he could feel the hot sweat rolling down his back and his hand was covered in gore and blood from holding the fingers.

He still had the fingers in his hand, in fact. Diego rolled down his window and tossed the digits out. "Take me to the restaurant."

Diego would need to gather everyone he could to find the chests, even if Enrique gave him the exact coordinates. There would be too much to move, too many prying eyes watching them at all times.

They arrived a few minutes later at the back parking lot of the restaurant, and Diego went inside flanked by his three bodyguards. Right to the bathroom, where he washed the blood from his hand and splashed water on his face.

He sat in his usual seat at his usual table, with his back to the wall. Waved at one of the waitresses, who would bring him a spread of food and drink. He would pick at it and then tell her to give the leftovers to the poor or someone who was hungry. Diego didn't care. He did it because it was the right thing to do.

Not right in the sense you needed to show mercy, but because it kept the peasants in line. The Wolf had taught him that move, and it seemed to work. Even though the locals knew he was a high-ranking member of the cartel, they tempered this with his generosity and the various gifts he gave to them.

Diego hated this small town. Too busy, too many eyes, but it was an important location for the north and south traffic, so he did his best to visit whenever he needed to.

The fact the plane had gone down six months ago meant it was even more important. Diego would reward the locals with a street fair soon, handing out millions of worthless pesos to them.

He wondered what he would do with Maria Guerrero now, too. He wanted her dead and knew she'd killed his brother, Raul. But she might be better used if she were alive long enough to help him claim the treasure.

Diego ate a taco but pushed the rest of the food away. He motioned for his bodyguards to eat, and they all took a sizable portion of the food.

"Waitress... take this away and give it to the poor," Diego said with a smile. "And add another dozen tacos to it as well as a good bottle of tequila."

She took the food away and bowed, never making eye contact.

I am a good person. I help the commoners and the low-lives, Diego thought.

His phone rang and he answered it.

"Enrique is dead. Too much blood loss. He said something about a beach but it was hard to know if that's what he really said, since his teeth were missing and his tongue was so swollen in the end," one of the torturers said.

Diego frowned. "Well, you did your best. I appreciate it. I will send the car back for all of you and we'll get you on the first plane out of Mexico. Clean up the scene and prepare the body for transportation. I thank you for your time and your work."

Enrique mentioned a beach. With nearly six thousand miles of beach, that meant it could be anywhere, Diego thought.

Of course Diego could shrink down the search area to the water right outside of this town, but it was still several miles. He would need more men and women, including Maria.

"Go back to the warehouse and kill the three men who screwed up, and bring me their bodies and also the body of Enrique. We'll need to find a suitable spot to dump and burn them, and hurry," Diego said to his bodyguards. "Then torch the warehouse."

TWO

Cuba sat up from bed as the morning sun glared through the useless window shades. His body was screaming at him that he had a hangover, but he thought himself too rugged to be slowed down from a long night of drinking, so he ignored it.

Men like him didn't get hangovers. They were for the weak.

Cuba stumbled toward the bathroom and winced as he flipped on the light. The brightness made a buzzing in his ear.

Today will be a good day at sea, and I will feel invigorated and strong, Cuba thought. *As soon as I have a cup of coffee with maybe a slug or two of rum in it.*

For the most part, last night was uneventful. Sure he'd had to have a talk with Alberto, who was most likely lying to him about the man now in the basement. He didn't know what Alberto was up to, but Cuba would have to make sure to keep an eye on him.

He'd also heard Grace walk in afterwards. He wanted to stop her and bring her into the kitchen. At that point, he was into his second bottle of scotch and was feeling emotional and wanted to attempt to connect to her in some way. She was his daughter, and from the way she screamed at Ernie Patek when he tried to take her, it appeared she was more on Cuba's side than the man who had raised her.

It just went to show how much of a stupid pig Ernie was. No daughter wanted that for a father. They wanted a strong, take charge, aggressive man. Qualities they would later look for in a potential spouse.

Now, in the morning light with his heart jackhammering, he scolded himself. The problem with drinking at night was that he tried to be too friendly with everyone. He should keep it professional. Then, if anyone was still alive after they found the treasure, they could all go out and get drunk and act stupid and buddy-buddy together.

He walked into the kitchen, where everybody was already there finishing their food and coffee. It was silent. Alberto was skirting around everyone, trying to avoid eye contact with him. Grace was just how she normally was. Didn't seem to have a care in the world. JoJo and Rick were sitting together, which stirred some jealousy in him.

Rick looked exhausted. He knew that he'd gone out last night, but if Cuba was up when he'd come home he didn't remember it. He would have to find out what time Rick had come back. He figured he was like a castrated bull at this point, with JoJo barely saying a word to him, and Cuba on the verge of taking her for himself. He was a harmless, broken man. But that didn't mean he couldn't be up to something.

Cuba had to give him credit for his attempted assassination on him. Even if it was with a flare gun. Normally, he would have had anyone shot immediately and tossed overboard, but this situation was different. Not only did he want to break down

JoJo's defenses and make her come to him, but he wanted to bring Rick from a man to a flea. To tear him down so much he turned into nothing.

The flare hurt, but not as much as standing there pretending to be fine and *not* killing him had hurt Rick.

Cuba grabbed a cup of coffee and, when nobody was watching, poured some booze into it. He was too wobbly on his feet to be of any use. Just a little bit would help clear that up. Not that he had a hangover or anything.

"Not much sleep, Alberto?" he asked just as the man was trying to slink out of the room.

Alberto stopped and Cuba saw his shoulders drop before he turned to face him.

"Too still on the land. I need a good night swell on the boat to rock me to sleep."

"Are you asking to be able to sleep on your boat instead of with us fine people?"

"No, just takes a little getting used to."

"I tell you what. You tell me what you said to that drunken buffoon at the bar, I'll let you stay on your beloved boat day and night. It'll be like you're free again."

"And what else? Have a guard standing over me the entire time to make sure I don't take off?"

"Nothing like that. That would be intrusive. I'd just have a bomb connected to the ignition so you blow to pieces if you try to start the boat when I'm not there."

"Sounds tempting, but I told you already. We just talked bullshit for a bit and I left."

"You're a man who sticks to his story. I like that."

"I stick to my word."

"Yeah. we'll see. Take the rest in the Jeep to the boat. The two of us will drive out shortly. Make sure they're ready for today's dive by the time I get there."

The guards he was talking to nodded and left, bringing JoJo, Rick, and Grace outside.

Once they shuffled out and the door closed, Cuba grabbed a random bottle of booze from the counter and gestured for Alberto to follow him.

"Do you know why I picked this house as my home base?" Alberto shook his head. "It's one of the few places around here with a basement. Being this close to the water, it's not the best idea to have one. Apparently, later in the season it tends to flood. But when you're in the business I am, having a basement is useful for many things. Storing weapons. Money. Drugs. But it's best for keeping people who piss me off."

Cuba led Alberto down the hall toward his bedroom. This area had been deemed off limits when he'd brought them here, and made sure a guard was standing in the hallway at all times. He didn't want any of them to get any ideas and try to kill him in his sleep. The basement had nothing to do with it.

But now, with two people down there, it was just another reason to keep everyone else away.

Cuba brought him to the basement door, which was locked with a five-digit code box.

"Turn away, please." Cuba entered the code and the lock sprung. "It's a good place to keep someone you need information from. Or someone you just enjoy torturing. As you can probably already tell, the smell is not the best. Moldy, mildewy, rank. It's not the kind of smell one can get used to over time. It lingers forever. It's like... passive torture. When I'm not down here they have to deal with that."

Cuba turned the corner at the bottom of the stairs and flipped on a switch. Against the wall, dirty and beaten, was Maria Guerrero, and the drunk idiot they'd picked up from the bar that Alberto had been talking with. Cuba didn't know the man's name because he had gone from making no sense at all, to what appeared to be full on delirium tremens.

The man was on his side, scratching at bugs that weren't there.

Cuba walked over and sat him up, slapping him a few times to get him to realize where he was. He poured some of the alcohol into the bottle cap and helped the man drink it. In a few minutes, his shaking seemed to become less severe.

"See this man? Alberto? You spoke with him at the beach. I want you to tell me what he told you. You tell me what he told you, and I give you the rest of this bottle. Then we just let you go, like nothing happened."

Cuba heard Alberto shuffle behind him. He glanced over to make sure he wasn't going to get hit in the head with anything. Though he'd had his men make sure anything that could be used as a weapon was taken out of the basement.

"Asshole," the man said.

"What?"

"He said he was working for an asshole. Then we had more drinks and–" Cuba saw the man's eyes shift to Alberto. "And we had shit-shat."

"Excuse me?"

"I told you," Alberto said. "We chit-chatted and I left. I didn't want to tell you the other part because I didn't need you getting upset. Maybe leaving out that detail was why you still think I'm lying to you."

Cuba stood up and looked between the two of them, then handed the bottle to the man on the ground.

"Fine. I'm an asshole. No surprise there. But when I find out what really went on, you're going to wish that's all I am. Now, let's go. We have some diving to do."

THREE

Ignacio was sitting in the sand not too far from where the treasure chests were located in the waves, not visible due to the high tide.

This was his quiet place, and it wasn't only because of so much wealth nearby. He had always loved the beach and loved the sounds of the ocean.

There was a calmness that came over him, and Ignacio couldn't find it anywhere else.

In the chaos of running his crew, he found a different comfort. Knowing he was doing things that helped others, his family and himself. It felt good to be on the move and getting things done.

But here, on the beach, everything else melted away. He could sit for hours and clear his mind of all of the many thoughts he had. Ignacio knew he was much older than his physical body. His mind wrapped itself around concepts and ideas no child his age should think about.

He was well-read and observant. While children his age should be worried about school work and playing video games or Pokemon cards, Ignacio thought like an adult. He didn't want to collect stupid cards; Ignacio was setting the foundation for the rest of his life.

I'm doing pretty good, considering I have a vast treasure only steps from me right now, he thought.

Ignacio knew there was work to be done but right now he just wanted to enjoy the quiet.

Birds circled overhead and he watched as they took turns diving into the ocean and snatching fish, flying away with their feast to eat.

He was getting hungry himself and decided he'd take out his fishing pole later today and catch some dinner for him and his mother. She would appreciate that, and he'd even help her to clean them.

Ignacio heard someone approaching on the beach and he turned and smiled.

It was Catalina, who gave him a wave.

"What are you doing here?" Ignacio went to stand but she waved him back down and joined him, sitting a few inches from him.

"I thought you'd be here," Catalina said with a smile. "I know you like to get away and come here."

The last time Catalina had been near this spot, she'd set Ignacio up with Arturo and Leo. They'd taken the crew from him and Catalina had shown her bad side.

He forgave her, if only because he had a real fondness for her.

Enough to let her know what sits only a few meters from this very spot? I'll need to think about it, Ignacio thought.

"What's on your mind today?" Catalina asked.

Ignacio shrugged. "I needed a break for a couple of hours. I wanted to put things together in my head, you know? I needed to stay focused."

"I'll leave you alone. Sorry," Catalina said and went to stand.

Ignacio took her by the hand and brought her gently down to the sand again, casually pulling her closer. "No. I'm glad you're here. I like spending time with you."

Catalina grinned and looked out to the water. "And I like spending time with you."

Another bird dove and caught another fish and they both laughed at the sight.

"How do you think this latest adventure will play out for us?" Catalina asked.

Ignacio wasn't sure, because the goal was to find the treasure, which he'd already done. All he could do now was feed bits of information to Cuba and Rick but never enough to have Cuba know where it was.

"With anything else... We'll do what we can do and hope for the best. I'm sure we'll be helpful enough that they will pay us well. One step closer to leaving this town." Igancio sighed. "As we get older we'll have to find other things to do with our lives. There are only two choices: work for the cartel or get away and start a new life."

"I fear we're all going to be working for the cartel," Catalina said. "Maybe they'll be nicer to us because of your aunt."

Ignacio shook his head. "Not likely. They only care about their bottom line. Family is a good tie, but when you work for the cartel they become your family. One and only. No, I am getting out as soon as I can." He thought of the treasure again and willed himself not to look in that direction.

"I'm sad because if you leave I will never see you again." Catalina put a hand on Ignacio's shoulder.

"Come with me." Ignacio said it before he thought about it, but he knew he was being honest. Truthful. He wanted Catalina in his life forever. "We can go together and have a wonderful life."

"I guess if we had the money and the means to do it, then sure," Catalina said and squeezed his shoulder. "But I think we'll be trapped here like everyone else."

"No, there is a way out of this for us," Ignacio said and stood up. "Let me show you."

He knew as soon as he said it this was wrong. This could not end well. Catalina could not be trusted, and she'd proven it in the past. But... Ignacio loved her. Wanted to show her there was a way for them to be happy. Now, not in five or ten years.

Against his better judgment he took Catalina by the hand and helped her up.

For a second, she was inches from his face. She was shorter than Ignacio, but he knew if he moved his head forward and down their lips would meet.

He could smell the shampoo in her hair. She was wearing a hint of perfume, too.

"Come with me," Ignacio said and turned away. His face was hot. She was so pretty. He knew someday he would ask her to marry him, and they'd have children together. A good life, away from this town and this country and the cartel.

Ignacio led her down to the water's edge and slipped off his shoes. Catalina looked confused but she took off her sandals.

"I need to show you this, but obviously you cannot tell anyone else," Ignacio said. "Swear. Promise me."

"I promise," Catalina said. "Just show me."

Ignacio waded into the ocean, gripping Catalina's hand and leading the way.

"There. See it?"

Catalina pulled away from Ignacio and rushed forward. "Wait, what is it? A chest? A treasure in the ocean? The one we're looking for?"

"Yes, the one we're looking for, except I had already found it." Ignacio smiled.

"Then we need to pull it out and see what's inside… or have you already done that?" Catalina put a hand under the surface and touched the chest.

"No, I haven't opened them yet. I don't know what's inside but I know it has to be valuable. They're too heavy to move, and stuck in the sand," Ignacio said.

"We'll get a crowbar and bust it open." Catalina was laughing and looked so happy.

"No. Not yet. We need to be cautious. The cartel is in town, a lot of them, and there are others, too. The man we're working for, Cuba, is very dangerous. He'll take it and kill all of us. Our families as well. For now we leave it where it is and see what happens," Ignacio said.

Catalina shook her head. "We need to devise a plan to get it off of the beach and somewhere safe."

"And we will. But for right now this stays between us. No one else needs to know, or this will be a giant mess," Ignacio said.

He wanted to cry because he knew this wasn't going to end well.

FOUR

JoJo looked out to the ocean. Cuba had wanted them in wetsuits and ready when he got there, but the day was too nice, and the breeze against her skin felt too good.

She never thought she would start to get sick of being in the water, diving every day for hours. She needed a break, but that wasn't an option. Not until they found the treasure or Cuba took them out. She would give anything to just stay where she was, with a beach chair and a cold drink, and let the spray speckle her body.

There wasn't much to do for any of them until Cuba arrived. Rick was rooting around on the boat deck, moving gear into place. He looked exhausted and, even though they hadn't really been talking, she got a feeling he was avoiding her for another reason.

JoJo could smell a secret from miles away. It was how she knew Grace was up to something, and now Rick was hiding something from her.

Now wasn't the time to approach him about it. Even back at Cuba's complex it would be a touchy situation to speak openly. Grace didn't seem too concerned about discussing things, but

JoJo had too many years of experience to not be naturally suspicious.

Either Cuba had the entire place bugged with hidden audio or video equipment, or there was absolutely nothing. He didn't seem the type to do something half-assed. Which meant, if she was being cautious, there was no place to keep a secret.

She could drag Rick into the bathroom and turn on the faucet and shower, hoping the noise would cover their voice. But she didn't know if that was just Hollywood shit, and after that mishap with Rick and the flare, JoJo wasn't going to take a chance.

She stood and wiped the sand off her legs and ass. Grace was already laying on the back of the boat, getting an even deeper tan. Give it a couple decades and she'd be really sorry about all the tanning. Or dead from skin cancer.

The two guards were taking turns watching Rick, the ocean, and Grace. Mainly Grace.

Fuck it, JoJo thought. *Why the hell can't I relax?*

She headed to the bar on the beach, the one she'd first talked to Alberto about their plans to get the treasure. Before Cuba or anyone else came into the picture and messed it all up.

She waited for one of the guards to try to stop her, to yell out, but nothing happened. They were too busy pretending to be guarding while staring at Grace's body. Maybe the girl could be useful after all. There was nothing to stop JoJo from walking straight past the bar and continuing on and disappearing.

Well, there were a couple things keeping her here. Rick and the treasure.

She'd been involved in the search for too long now to just give up on it. And with Rick, despite the loss of trust, which was slowly beginning to go away, she really did care for him. They'd been together for so long, and seen so many things, been involved in a ton of shady and fun situations, that the thought of him not being around made her sad.

Maybe that's why she was being so hard on him. Was it because of her selfishness of wanting him with her? Granted, anybody should be upset at an ex-addict who was straddling the fence. But he hadn't actually fallen over. And as much as she initially thought he could be lying about that, she was beginning to realize that he was telling the truth.

If he had fallen off the wagon, it would be obvious by now.

Which meant whatever he was hiding had nothing to do with that. Wherever he was going when he disappeared, it wasn't for drugs.

He must have a plan. And she'd have to find out what it was. By himself, he had good connections and was a decent fence, but together they were something special.

JoJo sat at one of the seats at the bar counter and ordered a beer. It wasn't the best idea to drink before going on a dive, but she really didn't care. She was tired of following everything Cuba said. She had a feeling everyone else was too.

Alberto had left the other day to do his boat checks, but she figured it was mostly to get away. Or it had something to do with Grace's plan. Rick and Grace both seemed to just wander off. Meanwhile, she was staying on the grounds, being a good little girl.

Well, fuck that. She never was one to let anyone else tell her what to do, so she wasn't going to start making that a habit now.

It seemed like Cuba's attempts at keeping everyone wrangled was simply falling apart.

"I remember you. Hard to forget," the bartender said.

"Oh yeah? How's that?"

"You were here a while ago, with Captain Alberto. I don't know what you two were discussing, but it must have been something good considering I've seen a bunch of you launch off the dock every day. Can you give me a hint?"

"Jimmy Hoffa. We're looking for his body."

The bartender chuckled and put away the glass he'd been wiping. JoJo couldn't help but notice how built he was. Not in an overstuffed-bag-of-marbles way, but lean with forearms like ropes. He wasn't too bad looking either, though his face reminded her of something she couldn't put her finger on.

"People come here, they're looking for sun. Drinks. Maybe something stronger. Nobody looks for dead bodies. We have people here who hide them well."

"The cartel. Yeah. They can be annoying."

"Seriously, what are all of you doing? And why the weapons? It's not that unusual to see men with guns, but with a few Americans in tow, it could mean bad business. We're a town trying to get more into the tourist game. Don't need any bad press."

"Just love the ocean. Diving. We heard there were pirates around here, so we hired some muscle."

"A good thing. You can never be too careful. Hopefully they're well-trained."

"The best in the biz." JoJo took another sip of beer. It had been so long since she'd had a cold one that her mouth grimaced at the bitterness of it.

"They can't be too good," the bartender said, coming from behind the counter.

"Why's that?" JoJo said. At least she thought she did. The beer was hitting her head very fast. She should have eaten more for breakfast.

"They appear to be dead."

JoJo turned, the world beginning to spin. Two bodies laying on the dock. A couple of other men with guns were aiming them at Rick and Grace. They were yelling back and forth, Rick gesturing in her direction.

One of the men shot into the air and leveled the gun back at Rick.

"You can never be too careful with who you're dealing with. Your boss, Cuba, needs to hire better security."

JoJo watched as Rick started the boat, still arguing, then took off into the ocean with Grace. She turned back to the bartender, who was now hovering over her, keeping her from falling off the chair.

"Who are you?"

"Diego Santiago. And I will be needing your help, JoJo."

FIVE

Cuba arrived at the dock and frowned. The boat was missing and so was his daughter and Rick.

Alberto and JoJo were leaning against a police vehicle and Cuba could see bodies covered by sheets. A slew of police and ambulance workers were swarming like ants over spilled ice cream.

"Should I even ask?" Cuba walked up to JoJo and Alberto, keeping an eye on the police. Not that he feared them, but he knew they would tell the cartel or anyone else anything they heard for a small price. No one in Mexico could be trusted.

Alberto waved his hand at the bodies. "The cartel. Killed your men. Kidnapped Grace and Rick. Would've killed me if I'd been on the boat. Same with JoJo."

Cuba turned to JoJo. "Why weren't you on the boat?"

"I was getting a drink while we stood around and waited for you to finally arrive... which you did nearly thirty minutes after we were attacked," JoJo said and frowned. "Where were *you*, huh?"

"I don't answer to you."

JoJo stabbed a finger into Cuba's chest. "And I don't answer to you. Remember that. Seems convenient you were so late, the first day you arrived so late, in fact. Conveniently when we were attacked. Anything you want to tell us, Cuba?"

Cuba wanted to slap her but knew it would ruin things with JoJo forever, and there were too many witnesses. Too many police. "I hope you're not serious. Why would I be working with the cartel? And letting them kidnap my daughter? It makes no sense."

"None of this has made sense in a long time, gringo," Alberto said.

Cuba wanted to punch him, too. Alberto was finally finding his balls thanks to JoJo, which was not a good thing. If everyone turned against Cuba, he'd have a hard time to let them believe he was going to let them live once they found the treasure. More than likely, they'd all plot against him. He needed them on his side, or to think they were all still on the same side.

"The last thing we need is the cartel involved," Cuba said. "I swear to both of you, I had nothing to do with this. If I was here they would've likely shot me, too. No, we need to think. Where would they take Grace and Rick?"

Alberto sighed. "The cartel owns everything, so they could go anywhere and feel safe. If I had to guess... they might want Rick and Grace to dive for them, thinking we're close to where we need to be to find the treasure."

Cuba nodded. "Then we have to assume the cartel knows what we're after and wants it. But then why not let us do all the work and simply take it from us?"

"Excellent question." Alberto shrugged his shoulders. He looked at JoJo like he wanted to ask a question, but kept his mouth shut. Cuba noticed JoJo looked away quickly.

There is something they aren't telling me, but I don't want to push it, Cuba thought.

He watched as the police did their thing, none of them coming over to ask any questions. Cuba supposed they'd seen this all a million times over the years. Just another cartel murder. Just another statistic.

"My boat is gone now," Alberto said. He was staring at Cuba. "I need my boat back or a new boat."

"Oh, okay." Cuba wanted to punch Alberto so badly right now. "I'll pull one out of my ass for you."

"As long as you clean it after you pull it out of your ass, I'm good," Alberto said.

Cuba turned away. "We need to get back to the villa. We're exposed out here, and if the cartel comes back these local police aren't going to help us. In fact, they'll let the cartel use their handcuffs and police vehicles to take us away."

The three of them got into the vehicle with Cuba driving. He had men back at the villa, so he'd feel safer there. No one could get inside without a small army, and Cuba knew the cartel was not going to make a full frontal assault, even though they'd killed his men here on the docks in broad daylight and kidnapped people and stolen their boat.

Cuba didn't care about what happened to Rick. The best-case scenario was Rick would be shot in the head and tossed into the ocean, never to be found. Fish food. JoJo would be upset but Cuba hadn't killed the man. Cuba would bide his time and be the comforting shoulder for her to lean upon, the soothing voice to calm her. The man to eventually win her heart.

Grace was another problem altogether.

If she was hurt, Cuba would have to kill anyone even remotely involved with her death. If these scumbag cartel drug dealers touched his little girl, he'd wipe them and their families out. He'd slaughter them back several generations, in fact. Scorched earth. Nothing of the cartel would remain, and he'd spend the rest of his life doing it.

"We need to reorganize and figure out where they're taking Grace and Rick," Cuba said. "Maybe we'll get lucky and they'll contact us with their kidnapping demands."

"How many men do you have left?" Alberto asked.

Cuba slammed on the brakes and wanted to cry.

Up ahead, at the end of the street, he could see his villa.

What was left of it, anyway.

The gate had been breached, a twisting hunk of metal in the road. The windows had all been shot out and even from this distance Cuba could see the bodies of his men on the ground.

He pulled into the compound and grabbed an automatic weapon, ready to rush inside and kill as many of the cartel as possible.

JoJo and Alberto were a few steps behind, also armed.

The villa had been ransacked, everything broken and ripped apart with gunfire. Blood on the walls and on the floor.

"No. This is not happening," Cuba said. He went from room to room but anyone he saw was dead. There were no cartel members that had been taken out, either.

"Check upstairs." Cuba pointed to JoJo and Alberto. "We meet back here in five minutes. Go."

Cuba went down to the basement, already knowing what he was going to find.

No Maria.

They took her. Right from underneath my hand, Cuba thought. The man that Cuba was sure had been conspiring with Alberto was also gone.

Cuba swung his fists in the air, wanting to punch everyone. Wanting to break shit. Wanting to get back in control.

"We need to leave. This isn't safe. I'm not sure if there is anywhere that is safe right now," Cuba said once he met up with JoJo and Alberto.

Cuba had no clue where they were going to go, but he knew he needed them to find the deepest hole possible to climb down into and lick their wounds.

He'd never been this defeated in his entire life, and the cartel was going to pay.

SIX

Rick didn't have a choice. He had to do what they told him. If he'd continued arguing, they would have shot him and tossed him overboard, and then taken off with the boat and Grace anyway.

He hated leaving JoJo behind, but figured it was better he followed orders now and stayed alive. He'd be no good to her dead.

Rick had driven boats before, but nothing quite as big and not in the open ocean. The two men onboard with them had programmed coordinates into the GPS and he did his best following the route.

He knew enough – hopefully – to get them there without tearing the bottom out of the boat, or letting a rogue wave capsize them.

Grace seemed unfazed by the situation. Though, she usually appeared that way. It was either a calm, almost zen-like attitude with her, or a crazy, screaming, psycho out of nowhere.

Rick looked back at her and she winked. Maybe the crazy psycho was always in there, just sometimes not as outspoken. He didn't understand how she could be so laid back when they were just hijacked and being brought to some undisclosed location. He didn't want to think what would happen to them once they arrived.

At least with Cuba, he knew they would stay alive until the treasure was found. Or until Cuba got frustrated enough and gave up. Getting taken by the cartel, which is who this most likely was, made his life going forward extremely unpredictable.

He'd had some training dealing with hostage negotiation when he was in the FBI, but nothing on how to try to save a life when you were the hostage.

They pulled into a dock and tied up. Rick hadn't seen beach houses or other landings for a while. Wherever they were, it was in the middle of nowhere. Or at least, far enough away that neighbors weren't going to see anything.

Or hear me scream, Rick thought.

There was a steep walk up the hill before they came out in the backyard where a nice house stood. There was a patio outside with furniture and a pool. Some people were sitting around on the chairs, while guards with automatic weapons walked the perimeter.

Grace passed Rick and headed to where the people were. Rick tried to stop her, but she dodged his grasp. He expected the guards to stop her, or worse, but they just made sure he kept walking while she moved ahead.

He saw someone stand and embrace Grace. What looked like introductions were made and she was given a drink.

When he got close enough, Rick recognized the figure. Ernie Patek.

What the hell is Ernie Patek doing here? He thought. *And is that the DEA agent who'd disappeared?*

"Rick, you've met my father, Ernie," Grace said as he approached everyone. "This is Baker. He's some kind of Fed. And this is Diego Santiago. I'm not exactly sure where he is on the cartel ladder, but he's up there somewhere."

Rick hesitantly shook the men's hands. Especially Patek. The last time he'd seen him, he was floundering in the ocean around a sinking boat.

"What are we doing here?" He was asking Grace, but Ernie spoke up.

"We've had ears on all of you shortly after Cuba started forcing everyone to find this treasure. Sure, there have been some hiccups, but I've been helping guide Grace so we can take Cuba down, and get the treasure at the same time."

"If there is treasure," Rick said.

"Oh, there definitely is. The problem is I have no idea where. I just know it's off the beaches of the town."

"So you've been working with Patek this whole time? Everything you've done and said has been fake?"

"Not everything," Grace said. "Most of it was pretty real. But we do know Cuba has the house bugged. He doesn't know that I know. I mean, anyone with half a brain would, at the least, act cautious in case it was. But one of Cuba's flaws is that he thinks he can read anyone. That he knows better than us. Never in a million years would he think I would act anyway but like the ditzy blonde he'd come to know. Run my mouth. Try to outsmart him."

Rick was starting to get an idea of what Grace was saying. He didn't know why he hadn't come to the realization sooner.

Everybody was pretty open about somehow getting out from under Cuba's grasp, but Grace was the most bold.

"You're feeding him bullshit, and he thinks it's real because he doesn't consider you a threat."

"Pretty much. Start talking about a plan to escape with the treasure once we find it. Get Alberto in, make him think it's real. You. Then, when you started getting all wonky, JoJo. There really was no method to it other than disinformation chaos. Cuba thinks I'm plotting against him. Alberto goes out with some made-up idea in his head, which only confirms we're moving against him. He starts spiraling, not knowing what to do since he needs all of us to continue searching."

"You break him down until he can't function in his right mind anymore. Starts seeing leprechauns and shit that isn't there. The paranoia winds up being his downfall."

"Exactly."

"Then why bring me here? Why tell me about this?"

"That was just how it panned out. You were on the boat. If JoJo had been there, she would have come. Both of you, if everyone had been on the boat."

"So she's fine, then?"

"Yes, she's fine," Diego said. He stood up and lit a cigar. "I had a talk with her. Had to give her a little sedative so she wouldn't do anything dumb and run after the boat. That would have been unfortunate, since my men would have had to shoot her. But she came to. It was a short-acting powder. I explained the situation, briefly. Made sure she understood, then left. As far as we know, she's fine."

"So where do we go from here? Besides someone giving me a drink and a seat so I can take this all in."

"Ransom us back to him. Or at least me. I don't know if he'd lift a finger to get you back," Grace said. "It has no meaning other than to just add another problem onto his table."

Rick saw a woman being walked past the sliding doors as Grace spoke. Her hands were tied, and her face was swollen.

"Is that Maria?"

"Yes. My men swarmed Cuba's house once he left. She was who I was after. All I wanted. Then Ernie filled me in on this treasure, and I agreed to lend him the help of my men and equipment for a cut. A little bonus on top of him finding my brother's killer."

"So what happens to us, then? Me and JoJo? Alberto?"

"See this through. Don't cause any problems, and you all walk. Pockets a little heavier than when you started," Ernie said.

"Yeah, I seem to be hearing those promises lately. They don't mean much of anything."

"I'm not in the habit of killing people just because they're loose ends. You get some money out of this, and you go and live your life knowing I won't come after you. Unless you try to fuck me."

Rick thought about the chest in the ocean. About Nacho. He'd be damned if this bastard was getting anything. He just needed to figure out how to get out of this new situation alive.

SEVEN

JoJo waited until Cuba had wandered off to secure them a room or rooms before she sidled up to Alberto. "We're going to be alright. I spoke with Diego Santiago. He was in the bar, right before the kidnapping."

"Who?" Alberto was watching Cuba at the registration desk. "I don't know if my heart can handle anymore of this, JoJo. I am an old, feeble man."

"You're not that old." JoJo didn't want to ask Alberto how old he was, because she had the sickening feeling they were closer in age than she would've liked. "As long as we play our parts with Cuba we'll survive."

"Then Grace and Rick are fine?" Alberto asked.

"Yes. Ernie Patek is behind this."

Alberto shook his head. "Then I don't think we're as fine as you think we are."

Cuba waved for them to join him.

"Go with the flow," JoJo said to Alberto.

They followed Cuba outside and past a swimming pool area and then down a tree-strewn path to a set of bungalows.

"It's not much but I paid cash for it, and we should be safe until more men arrive on the next flight," Cuba said.

JoJo frowned. "Wait... you rented us one bungalow? For all three of us?"

"I had no choice. This is the best option right now," Cuba said. His eyes were bloodshot and he looked awful. "Until I can find these cartel bastards and kill each and every one of them, and then kill their children and their pets and–"

JoJo put a hand up. "Calm down, Cuba. You're going to overheat and not be helpful. You need a drink. I'll go grab us a bottle of rum and we can talk."

Cuba grabbed her arm, fingers digging into her skin. "No. No one gets out of my sight until people start to die. Understand? You are both my prisoner until further notice." He lifted his shirt and JoJo saw the Glock in his waistband.

"Fine. Whatever. Show me to this mansion you've rented for us," JoJo said.

Cuba unlocked the door and waved for them to enter, which they did.

The cabana was cute but small. One bed, one couch. Thin flooring covering the ground.

"Obviously, the bed is mine," JoJo said.

"We share it." Cuba stalked around, even though it was a single room with a small bathroom in one corner with only a bamboo wall separating it.

"I'm not going to sleep with you," JoJo said. She pointed at Alberto. "The boys can have the bed and I'll crash on the couch."

Cuba spun around at her and his hand went to his weapon but he didn't pull it. "Are you going to argue about the stupid things that don't matter? We have bigger problems now. They are after us and we need to be diligent. We need to fight them. Go on the offensive."

"Have you ever heard the expression to not sweat the small stuff?" JoJo asked. "And it's all small stuff?"

"That is stupid," Cuba said and sat down on the couch. He ran his hands through his greasy hair and then rubbed his eyes. "I am so tired of all of this."

"We could walk away. There likely isn't even a treasure to find. Ernie Patek is probably dead, killed by the cartel," JoJo said. She sat on the edge of the bed and wondered if she'd need to wrestle Cuba for his Glock at some point. The man seemed very unstable right now.

"Then I will avenge my old friend. This is no longer about the treasure, this is about revenge. About pride. No one does this to me and gets away with it." Cuba stood and began pacing the small room.

Alberto, standing near the door, raised his eyebrows at JoJo.

This is all about ego, JoJo thought. *Cuba had been shown to be a fool, and the cartel had made quick work of him. Taken his daughter and killed all of his men. Destroyed his villa and showed Cuba he wasn't as much of a bad ass as he thought he was. For someone like Cuba, that was too far. He might never recover.*

"Then we sit and wait until your men arrive? How long will that be?" Alberto asked in a calming voice.

Cuba stopped pacing and pointed at Alberto. "When they get here they get here. I have some flying in and some crossing the border from Texas as we speak. Thirty men. Once they arrive we'll show out and let the cartel know we mean business. Then we'll get a new boat. Maybe once we kill the cartel in town we can take one or two of their boats."

"The cartel are cockroaches, sir. You will never be able to kill all of them, and openly starting a war with the Sinaloa Cartel will also put you on the radar of other cartels," Alberto said.

Cuba smiled but it wasn't pleasant. "Good. The enemy of my enemy is my friend, right?"

Alberto shook his head. "No. Right now there is an uneasy truce between many cartels, and they all rely on this cartel to move their product over the borders into Texas and California. Bringing so much heat and publicity to them would be disastrous."

Cuba waved his hand. "That's not my problem. I need them exterminated like the cockroaches they are."

Alberto glanced at JoJo and raised his eyebrow again.

"I need a shower." JoJo also needed time away from Cuba, hoping he'd eventually calm down and see his plan, what little of it there actually was, meant a death wish for all of them.

I need to get in touch with Ernie and Diego, my new allies, JoJo thought.

"Then take a damn shower." Cuba sat on the couch again but popped back up a second later and began his pace of the small room. "All we can do is wait. We all need to stick together and get through this. That's the only way."

JoJo had no clothes with her. She didn't remember when she'd showered last, but knew her undergarments likely stunk from her sweating. She went into the bathroom area and turned on the shower, groaning when it was only warm water. Not even hot enough for a proper shower.

Still in her clothes, she stepped under the spray and closed her eyes, letting the water soothe her.

She needed this right now. The last couple of hours had been a whirlwind, and she knew it was only going to get worse. Did Ernie and Diego even know where she was right now?

Diego had told JoJo to stay with Cuba and keep an eye on him to report back at a later time, but she hoped it also meant they had eyes on them, too.

We might truly be alone with this madman, JoJo thought.

There were no towels to dry off, so JoJo stepped back into the main room and was going to tell Cuba she needed to step outside and let the sun dry her. Maybe she could relax by the pool for a bit.

Alberto was smiling. He held a broken lamp in his hand.

"What did you do?" JoJo stared at the unconscious body of Cuba lying on the floor. "Did you kill him?"

"No. I am not a killer," Alberto said.

JoJo saw Cuba's chest rising and falling. He was still alive but he had a nasty-looking bump on the top of his head.

"He wouldn't shut up about killing little children. It was too much. I might be a simple fisherman, but I have family in the cartel. He was threatening them." Alberto shrugged and put the broken lamp back down on the side table. "When he turned away, I wasn't even thinking. I hit him with the lamp."

JoJo took the Glock from Cuba's waistband.

"Are you going to kill him, ma'am?" Alberto asked.

She realized she was pointing the weapon at Cuba. "I should but I won't. He'll come to and he's going to be really angry. I think it's time we left and found a new hiding spot."

"I know just the place. Follow me," Alberto said and opened the cabana door.

EIGHT

Maria didn't know what was going on at this point. She'd been betrayed and handed off to Cuba, who had his guards humiliate her the entire time she was in the basement. Next thing she knows, there's gunshots and yelling coming from upstairs. Cartel men, some she recognized, burst into the basement and, just when she thinks she's saved, they tie her hands and drag her to the back of one of the cars.

After spending what felt like hours in the trunk, being hit in the head by random objects and flung against the sides around turns, the car stopped.

It would have been almost better if she hadn't recognized where she was when the trunk opened.

The last significant time she'd seen Diego Santiago as lovers was when she was throwing him out of her bedroom, cursing and hitting him with any loose item at hand. He was laughing on his way out of the door, calling her a crazy witch.

Shortly after, his brother was moved to her crew and assigned as her second-in-command. It didn't take brains to figure out who pulled those strings.

She killed Raul, everything went to shit, and now she was staring at the front of Diego's beach house. A house she knew well. They'd spent many nights having fun in the bedroom, the pool, the den. Pretty much every room in the house except the laundry room.

Wait, she thought. *Even the laundry room.*

A man grabbed her roughly by the arm and pulled her toward the house. Maria didn't bother resisting. There was no point. Whatever was going to happen would happen. She could only hope she'd either be able to talk her way out of anything bad, or figure out a way to escape.

Diego liked to chat with his victims. That was a good thing for her. She never understood what he got out of it. It wasted time, and gave an opportunity for the person to extend their life. Maria just killed people. No words and no hesitation.

This could only be about one thing: Raul. Diego wouldn't have dared treat her this way for any other reason. Which meant her being grabbed wasn't approved by the higher ups. Which meant if she somehow managed to get out of this alive, she would only need to take care of Diego and whichever men remained loyal to him.

She walked in and the first thing she noticed was nothing had changed. Same furniture, same garish decorations. Same Diego.

Maria didn't have to be told where to go. She had personally dragged people, kicking and screaming, to the room Diego used as a holding area. If he was feeling generous, he wouldn't keep her in there too long. Considering the last time they were together and Raul's death, she wouldn't be holding her breath.

She glanced out the window as they passed the patio and saw Ernie, Baker, Diego, Rick, and Grace outside all standing around chatting like it was some high school reunion.

What the fuck is this? She thought.

Her eyes met Rick's for a moment and she tried to give him an inquisitive look, but her face was so swollen from Cuba's men that she didn't think it moved at all.

That changed things. Maria had no idea how any of them would have hooked up with Diego, but just Ernie being there may mean that she might not be in as bad a condition as she thought. Of course, Ernie had also been the one to hand her over to Cuba.

All of this was too confusing. She needed to sit, calm down, and gather herself together. Otherwise, she'd wind up spiraling into a never-ending train of bad thoughts.

Maria was asleep when Diego came into the room. The floor was made of roughly spread concrete with nothing between it and her. She sat upright and could feel the pockmarks on her arm and side of her face.

Since there was no light, Diego held an electric lantern, which he turned up and put in the middle of the room. He also brought in a chair and sat, staring at her.

"What do we do now, Diego?"

"Like in the past. Champagne. Food. Music. Some dancing. What should we do?"

"Raul was coming for me. If you didn't approve it, you had to at least know about it. You would have done the same thing."

"And I would have had that man's family after me, like you."

"This is your choice, not the cartel's. You can change your mind without losing any face."

"But I can't get my brother back."

Maria sighed and leaned against the wall. They were dancing, just with words.

"You didn't even really like Raul. Do you know how many times I saw you and him fight it out over something stupid? How many times have you told me in the middle of the night that you thought you'd be better off without him? You were thinking of doing the same thing. Why do I deserve punishment for following through with something you, deep down, wanted?"

"I was his brother," Diego yelled. "I'm allowed to kill him."

"Don't call my mom a bitch, only I can call my mom a bitch?"

"Exactly. You had no right. If you had a problem with him, you could have come to me."

"Bullshit, Diego. How long has it been? I know how long. Do you know why? Because I know how old our son is. I know what day he was born on. I've been there for every birthday. And I've been there when he's asked my sister who his father is. My sister, who he thinks is his mother. I swore when you left me, alone and pregnant, I would never come to you for anything ever again."

"What does any of this have to do with my brother? With how you brutally killed him, in public, to die shamefully in front of peasants?"

"Don't you see, everything has to do with you? That's how you've always been. All the things that happen in the world have to do with Diego Santiago. Maybe for once, take a seat and see how things really are. I think that, in your mind, I killed Raul because of some misplaced anger at you. I killed Raul because he was a backstabbing bastard who would have taken me down if I hadn't acted first. And if I go to the heads with this, they will stand on my side, not yours."

"What makes you think you're going to make it out of this house?"

Maria leaned forward, looking Diego in the eyes. She was sure she'd seen some hesitation when she mentioned she was in the right to kill Raul. If he was going to kill her, he'd need to be absolutely sure that none of the other people involved in taking her to him would open their mouths about it.

One cartel leader killing another was forbidden. Sure, it happened in the past, but the person who was left alive was not alive for long.

Maria had this leverage on him, and despite Diego being so sure of himself, she knew that he was afraid of the head of the cartel. The top dog. Someone others only saw when they were looking at the last second of their life.

"I will leave this house alive, Diego. Because you love yourself above anything else, and you will not risk your life just to take mine. But we may be able to solve this in a way that works for both of us. So that this little incident never gets out. Let me tell you a story about the last couple weeks."

NINE

Catalina liked Ignacio, and she believed he could get her out of this town. Out of Mexico. Out of poverty and gangs and cartels.

She also believed in herself, and doing what was right for her and her family above all else.

While Ignacio was big on talking about them all being a family, and doing for the crew first, Catalina knew that was the wrong way to look at it.

The only way to get ahead in this life was to be selfish and worry about yourself. Do what you need to do to get not only by but ahead, too.

"I have something to tell you. I need your help," Catalina told Arturo. "When you are well enough we have something to do. Something that will change our lives forever. Are you with me?"

Arturo stared at Catalina. He still looked weak but he'd been getting better each day. "Tell me what it is."

"Not until you promise not to tell anyone else," Catalina said. "I have a life-changing favor to ask you. I need to know we're on the same page and you won't involve anyone else unless absolutely necessary."

Arturo groaned. "Just tell me already."

Catalina shook her head. "Forget it. I should have known you would be too impatient. You'll never be able to keep this secret, and that's fine. I'll just rely on Ignacio with it."

Arturo grabbed her by the hand when she turned to leave his room. "Wait... does Ignacio already know about this, or are you coming to me first?"

"I came to you first. I found something and I need help moving it, before someone else finds it," Catalina said. She knew mentioning Ignacio would get Arturo wound up, which was the plan. If nothing else, Arturo had a one-track mind and wanted so desperately to be better than Ignacio.

She knew Ignacio was a better leader, a better person and a better soul than Arturo would ever be. Which was why she'd come to Arturo, because she knew what had to be done in the end.

"I promise I will help you and I will keep my mouth shut," Arturo said.

Catalina smiled. She knew he'd never refuse her request. Like Ignacio, Arturo wanted to be her boyfriend. They both thought they were in the lead and winning her heart. Catalina knew what men were really for, and it was only to provide for them, to protect them and be their servant.

She'd learned that from her mother and the many men her mother had had in and out of her life. Now that Catalina was older, she knew how to play the game better and better. Ignacio and Arturo were the first two but they would not be the last.

"The treasure we are supposed to help find for those men? I know where it is." Catalina smiled.

"Where?"

Catalina shook her head. "I'll have to show you when you are ready. We'll need to figure out how to move it, too, because there are several chests filled with gold and silver. Jewelry. So much more."

While she hadn't opened the chests and Ignacio said he hadn't either, she knew what they meant. Loaded with untold wealth. The way out of Mexico.

"How can we move it? The way you describe it... it seems like there might be too much for two children to do it," Arturo said.

"We are no longer children, and we will be able to do it. We just need to be patient. If we crack open the first chest and figure out how much is in there and what it weighs, we should be able to use a couple of milk crates and something with wheels to move it. Even if it takes us a week, it will be worth it." Catalina smiled. "I trust you. Think on how to do this, only the two of us, while you recover."

"I can go now," Arturo said. He sat up slowly in his bed. "I'm ready."

"No, not yet. Soon but not today. I trust you will start to work your way to full health, because this will change our lives. Our family's lives, too." Catalina stroked Arturo's chin with her finger and loved that his face grew red as she did it. "Get well. Quickly."

"Don't involve Ignacio. I can handle this," Arturo said. "I promise."

"And I believe in you," Catalina said and left.

She hoped in the future Ignacio would be able to forgive her. She might even give him some of the treasure, since he'd been the one to find it. What did they call it... A finder's fee? Catalina thought that sounded right.

Ignacio had made it perfectly clear he didn't want to open the chests or do anything until he'd thought it out more. To Catalina, that was stupid. The only thing they could do was move the treasure before someone else found it.

It's not like it's hidden away, it's within sight on a beach, Catalina thought.

At first, she'd thought about telling her mother and seeing if one of her boyfriend's would be interested in helping, but Catalina had decided against it. Those men were all thieves to begin with, low-level cartel soldiers stuck in this town.

They'd take it for themselves or alert the cartel about it.

Catalina needed Arturo, because he was impatient. In a few days he'd tell her he was ready. She didn't need him at one hundred percent. It would be better if he was still hurting, because she knew what she had to do once the wealth was moved to a safe location.

Arturo would then need to die to keep the secret safe.

Catalina would never hurt Ignacio, but she would also never tell him she was the one who'd taken the chests for herself. With any luck, he'd go to the beach and see the remains of the chests. Think someone had wandered by, randomly, and gotten into them.

I still need to figure out how to get my mother and I out of town in one piece, Catalina thought.

The problem with her mother was simple: she needed a man in her life in order to feel like she had worth. Even if she was suddenly very, very rich. She'd still need a man to tell her she was pretty and all the other sappy things that made her smile.

Catalina also worried that her mother would start spending the money they got from the treasure on more and more cocaine and marijuana. The only times her mother wasn't high was when she couldn't afford drugs and was between awful men.

One thing at a time. I need to secure a place to store the treasure, and then get Arturo moving to help me move it, a small portion at a time, over several nights. Then, when it is all accounted for and in my possession, I will have to deal with Arturo, Catalina thought.

Until then… she'd need to be extra nice to Ignacio and do whatever the crew needed to be done.

Catalina almost felt guilty for what she was going to do to her good friend, Ignacio. Almost.

TEN

Alberto wasn't sure what to do now that Grace wasn't around. Obviously, the plan was on hold since she was the leader and the only one who knew exactly what it was. He'd made sure he could use his friend's boat. His friend who was hopefully not still in the basement of Cuba's ruined home.

He'd left but come back, aware he needed a better plan.

Now JoJo was talking about some other plan involving Ernie Patek and the cartel. He was even more confused now. Should he be sticking with Grace or JoJo? Or ignore them both and stay with Cuba?

The same Cuba who was now snoring next to him. Alberto had gone from not knowing the man to sleeping in the same bed.

He got up from bed and walked into the next room, the only other room in the small house. As a charter captain, he was used to getting up with the sun and listening to the seagulls. But it was different here. The ocean was far enough away that he couldn't hear anything other than the occasional car passing by the place.

Alberto has spent his adult life trying to stay away from the cartel and people like Cuba. He dabbled with some smuggling, but never got himself into the situation he was in right now. With everybody now involved in this treasure hunt, he might as well have joined the cartel. At least he'd actually be making money instead of searching for hypothetical riches.

Alberto thought about that street rat for the first time since they'd handed him over to the hospital after getting shot. Nacho. That was his name. He wondered how he was doing.

Rick had seemed to be close with the kid. At least close enough to have the kid do some of his legwork for things. He seemed like a useful kid. Alberto wouldn't have minded him helping him out on the boat.

But the kid was probably scared straight after that bullet. Sitting in his house, studying or some crap. It took a certain type of person to live that kind of life. Most of the street rats never made it beyond that point. When they got old enough, they got legit jobs and sat around at night on the weekends talking about their bad-ass days when they were young.

Alberto knew all about that.

He'd run the same streets in his youth, along with Maria Guerrero, who'd blown up his boat and tried to kill him. Almost killed Nacho, also.

Back then, Maria had been just as beautiful. He'd had a giant crush on her, but was always afraid to say something. She may have been young, but she wasn't innocent. She'd always had that look on her face that would cause grown men to get nervous when they attempted to hit on her, or make fun of her.

Also, she was always hanging around with that Diego Santiago bastard. He was never part of the street kids. The guy had been connected and running for the cartel back then. It was like he'd skipped the right of initiation that most kids had to go through, and went straight to the big leagues.

There were rumors about killings and brutal torture which, if true, would make Diego a serial killer as a child. Who knew what he was now. Alberto assumed he was still with the cartel. A man like that could never go straight.

Alberto's thoughts went back to what JoJo had told him. The cartel had orchestrated the kidnapping of Grace and Rick. Apparently, a fake kidnapping. Now the two of them were working with the cartel to take down Cuba and the treasure.

Most people would put their money on the cartel, but Alberto had seen how Cuba operated. He wouldn't put anything past the guy.

He was still deciding what road he would take when Cuba walked into the room, stretching, and pouring himself a cup of coffee.

"What's wrong? I'm not a cuddly bed-mate?" Cuba asked.

"I've been with better. You should have taken the floor. JoJo would have been a better choice to cuddle with."

"If she'd chosen the bed, you would have been the one on the floor."

Cuba sat at the table and sipped his coffee. Alberto took him coming into the room just as he was trying to pick a side as some kind of a sign. There really was no winning no matter what, but he needed to choose which side would give him the best option of keeping his life when everything was said and done.

Alberto sat.

"We have an issue."

"No shit," Cuba said.

"No, I mean we have a real issue." Alberto glanced at the doorway to make sure JoJo wasn't standing there. "What happened at the beach? The boat and Rick. Your daughter. It was staged. They're working with the cartel."

"Bullshit. Rick I can see. He's a dead man either way. But Grace? You saw how she was screaming at Ernie. The girl wants to be with us. There's no way she'd go through all that and then suddenly flip on me."

"I think she may have been faking it. I should have told you sooner, but she was planning an escape. I'm not sure how real it was, now that I know what she's up to. But she had involved me. I thought, at the time, that it was a good idea. I see now that it is better to stick with you. I should have told you sooner, but I was afraid and trying to look out for myself."

Cuba stared at Alberto, then nodded.

"And the man you were talking to at the bar? The one who's probably dead in the other house's basement? Just chit-chat?"

"I was talking to him to ask how much he would charge if I needed to take his boat on short notice. He had the same boat as the one we're taking out every day for the treasure hunt. Part of Grace's plan was to do some kind of weird switch of the boat. I don't know. I didn't get the full details. Something about *The Count of Monte Cristo*?"

"The sandwich?"

"The book. Something about tricking guards. I don't know. It was probably all lies anyway."

"I appreciate your honesty. Now. I don't appreciate the lies. But I need you still. And if you are honest with me going forward, fully honest, I still promise you to leave with your life and a little something extra when this is done."

"I can do that. Now that I know where my allegiance should be, you can count on me for whatever you need."

"Good. For now, let's wake JoJo and get ready. We may have had a setback, but that doesn't mean we're not going out this morning."

"I'm already up."

Alberto jumped at the voice behind him. JoJo was standing in the doorway, looking like she'd just woken up. But who knew how long she'd been there. Or hiding and listening to their conversation.

Alberto decided he didn't care what she heard. She was now outnumbered. Her hopes for Rick to rescue her had just gone down the drain.

ELEVEN

Rick needed to get back to Nacho. They needed to formulate a plan to move at least some of the treasure. Maybe they'd have enough to escape this town. Maybe even enough to get out of Mexico.

This was all getting too hot to handle. Diego was a definite wild card, and Rick knew he had even less of a chance of surviving with Diego than Cuba.

Diego didn't need him. Not at all. He had an entire cartel to use to find the treasure, and it would only be a matter of time before he'd be able to locate it.

The cartel could use airplanes, boats, drones, foot soldiers and force everyone in the town to search for the treasure chests. Right now the only good thing was everyone thought they were sunken off the coast in a lot of water, unable to be seen from above.

All it will take is one drone flying over the beach, Rick thought.

It was so confusing right now, too. Who was really a friend and who was using him? Likely everyone was being used by everyone else.

Rick imagined the massive gunfight at the end of all of this, once the treasure was found by the group.

People were going to die. Maybe all of them, in fact. He couldn't see where they all sat down with smiles and split the treasure evenly, everyone getting a fair share.

He assumed there was more than enough to go around, but he couldn't think of one person in this group who wasn't greedy.

Rick included himself in that, too.

If given the chance he'd take out everyone but JoJo to secure the wealth. He tried to deny it but it was no use. Why be the better person, when no one else was going to be?

He knew Grace would do it. Easily. Already, she was acting like Ernie was the world's greatest dad, even though Rick had watched her do the same thing to Cuba.

She was a snake, and Rick had always known it but she was proving it right before his eyes.

Grace had a power and she was going to get far in life, because she only cared about herself. She only did things that were right for Grace. He was envious of her, truth be told.

Rick wanted to only care about Rick. It would be easier this way. He could sneak out, find an ax and chop through the treasure chests in the middle of the night. Steal as much treasure as he could and disappear into the night. Find a captain with a boat to get him north. Hire an Uber to the airport. Rent a car and cross into Texas and be gone.

He wished JoJo was here now, without Cuba. He'd need to see where her loyalty was and if they had a future together. Rick would never threaten JoJo or kid himself he'd ever harm her, but if she hesitated or told him flat-out they were done, he'd have no choice but to walk away.

It would kill him. He knew he'd be on a downward spiral and likely start using again, but nothing would even matter at that point.

JoJo might be the only good thing in his life, but Rick felt like he'd blown it with her.

He walked to the front door of the villa but one of the guards lifted his assault rifle and told him to stop.

"Am I a prisoner? Really? I just want to take a walk down to the beach and see the stars," Rick said, taking another step.

"I will shoot you. Orders." The man raised the rifle and aimed it at Rick's head.

Rick heard someone walking up behind him and turned to see Diego, smiling.

"Am I a prisoner?" Rick asked.

"Of course you are. We're all prisoners, aren't we? Whether it's because of our position in life, our station, or economic insecurity, the color of our skin, our religious or political beliefs, or just because someone above us doesn't like or trust us... prisoners we are," Diego said.

Rick wanted to punch Diego, but knew he'd be shot before he could make a fist.

"Let's take a walk," Diego said to me. Rick noticed he motioned for the guard to follow. "You want some fresh air? To see the beautiful water? We'll go to the back of the house. The breeze is nice this time of night. Stars above, too."

Rick was led by Diego, who had a firm grip on his shoulder. It was beautiful outside, and the two men – followed by an armed guard – walked down to the dock, where a couple of boats were moored.

"How well do you know Ernie Patek and Maria Guerrero?" Diego asked.

Rick shrugged. "Not well. There aren't many people I really know, especially in Mexico."

"But you do know JoJo, which is good." Diego stopped walking and faced Rick. "I learned a long time ago not to trust anyone, never completely. Always keep something of yourself back. Secrets but also things that make you tick. No? Especially when it comes to women."

"Like you and Maria?" Rick asked, knowing he might be kicking a hornet's nest but not really caring at the moment. His thoughts kept straying to how close he was to the treasure. No one else. If he could manage to break away from Diego and his cartel thugs, he might be able to escape with riches.

Diego laughed. "Yes, like Maria and I. She is beautiful. She was even more beautiful in her younger, more exciting days. Before she became so hard and callous. Inside of her is that young girl I fell in love with, and I'm hoping to reconnect with on some level."

"She killed your brother," Rick said.

"And gave me a son. I think you even know him." Diego was smiling. "You've paid him from time to time to help gather information."

Rick felt like he'd been punched in the gut. He knew Maria was likely Nacho's mother but had no clue who the father was. Until right now. "I know him in passing."

"My sources tell me you always treat him with respect. I want to tell you I appreciate that, Rick. I do." Diego held out his hand and Rick shook it.

"He's a good kid. I call him Nacho."

Diego laughed. "I bet he hates that. Keep calling him the funny name, because it will build his character. I don't even want to tell you what the other children called me growing up. It made me angry and made me hard. I took care of myself on the streets because of it."

Rick could only nod. He worried this was the end of the line for him. Had he crossed Diego by calling Ignacio Nacho? Did Diego think it racist, or was the thought of his son being made fun of enough to have Rick killed?

"Ignacio will no longer be a part of this. Understand? It is time for him to move on. In fact, I'm going to move him and his mother..." Diego frowned. "Maria's sister, but you get it... they will be coming here. You can stay friendly with my boy but nothing more. I will be keeping tabs on you and on him. If I see anything more than a casual hello, I will strip your body of flesh, slowly and painfully, and string you up by your arms in the center of town. As a warning."

Rick nodded. "I'll keep my distance." He realized Diego was making this easy by reuniting him with Nacho, but also making this infinitely harder because he'd also be a prisoner of Diego and the cartel.

TWELVE

Ignacio had heard the gunshots from his house. Even still, on his shitty bike, he'd made it to the house before the cops. They were all on the dole, anyway. If this was the cartel that rushed that asshole Cuba's giant place, the cops would know to take their time until it was sure there were no cartel men still there.

The last thing any of them wanted in this town was to lose the money they got paid under the table to ignore, or at least downplay, the cartel's moves.

He stood on the beach and watched as the stragglers of men left the house, taking their plunder before the cops showed up. It wasn't lost on him that Cuba's house was being looted for its expensive items while an unknowable amount of treasure chests were hidden just down the beach from him.

Ignacio sat, watching the house and eating a plantain and peanut butter sandwich. He'd seen a biography on television about it being Elvis's favorite food. Elvis used bananas, but it was basically the same thing. If there was anyone in the world who was the picture of cool, it was Elvis. His music wasn't that great, but the guy knew how to make all the girls weak in their knees.

Ignacio thought about Catalina. If he was like Elvis, he wouldn't be in this weird situation where he thought she liked him, but at other times wasn't sure. He didn't understand girls. It seemed like they were all nice when they wanted something, and then when they got it they ignored him.

The sirens were getting louder. Ignacio was about to leave when the side door of the house burst open. Two men walked quickly across the street onto the beach. Ignacio sat and turned to face the ocean. He tried to look like some dumb kid without a care in the world.

The men took off their hats and zipped up their jackets to hide the guns in their belts. The cops drove by, yanking into the driveway, along with a fire truck. The authorities ran into the house, guns drawn.

The two men chuckled and one brought out a cell phone.

"All clear. The bitch wasn't lying. Some drunk was in the basement trying to suck out the last drop of booze." The man paused.

Ignacio tried to make his ears bigger so he wouldn't miss anything. Whatever had happened at Cuba's definitely had to do with the treasure.

"Shot him. The guy was useless. Couldn't understand a word he was saying. Even if we brought him and he sobered up, his brain is probably too water-logged to remember anything." The men listened again. "He said nothing about Maria. I don't think he even knew what was going on."

The man put the phone into his pocket as they passed Ignacio. He glanced down at him and frowned.

"Shouldn't you be in school or something?"

"It's the summer. No school."

Ignacio had no doubt this guy had done his share of skipping classes in his day. Most likely didn't graduate. Most people who made a living as muscle couldn't spell Mexico.

Usually, he would have given the guy more shit. Thrown some insults at him. Those guys wouldn't shoot a kid. Well, they would, but only if they were told.

But hearing the name Maria threw Ignacio off his game. He wanted the men out of his sight because his brain was spinning.

When they took off, he headed to town. He needed to get to his mother's house to see if Maria was there. She usually showed up around this time, and if not definitely called to check in.

It couldn't be her, he thought. *How would she have gotten taken to Cuba's house? As a prisoner. They must have meant some other Maria.*

But Ignacio knew better. He let himself hope that the cartel had destroyed Cuba's place as a rescue mission to get Maria back, but the way the man had called her a bitch on the phone said otherwise.

He tried to act natural when he got home and asked his mom about his aunt. His mom was smart, though, and even though she might not know yet that Maria was in trouble, Ignacio could tell she saw through his facade.

"Why are you so worried about your Aunt Maria? Are you getting bored being with your Mama?"

"No, it's just that she hasn't been around lately. You know she's my favorite aunt."

"She's your only aunt."

"Still my favorite. When was the last time you talked to her, anyway?"

His mother stopped stirring the sauce on the stove. Whatever Ignacio had to do to help out Maria, he was damn sure going to eat some of his mother's cooking before he did it.

An hour later, he left with a lump of food in his stomach and a lump of worry in his throat. He didn't even know where to start. He could call on some of his crew, but they would be lost as well. Where does a kid go to find their cartel boss family member?

Rick would know. If Ignacio could find Rick, he'd be able to help find Maria.

But the last time he'd seen Rick, he'd been sneaking in and out of the same place Maria was being held. He knew he wasn't dead in the house, since he'd seen Rick drive by on the way to the beach earlier in the morning.

The beach. That was where he should be headed.

Ignacio looked around for Alberto's boat when he got to the dock. He'd only been familiar with the boat he was on that got blown up after he got shot, but he'd glanced at Cuba and everyone else getting on the new one. He was sure he'd know when he saw it. And hopefully it wouldn't be empty.

They must still be out looking for the treasure, he thought. *They probably don't even know the house was a shit show.*

Ignacio sat on the dock, his feet dangling just above the water. He wondered if sharks could get this close to the shore. He didn't need to lose his feet to some maneater.

"Hey, kid. You waiting for Captain Al and that pendejo he's chartering out to who-knows-where every day?"

The man who owned the bar stood behind him.

"Yeah. Do you know when they'll be back?"

"They never went out. Some piece of shit hit me in the back of the head and stuffed me in the storage closet. Heard gunshots and the boat rushing off. When I got out, I saw Alberto and that asshole, some hot older woman, all standing around yelling. No boat, though."

"Was the woman's boyfriend with her? A gringo who looks like he's miserable?"

"No. From what I overheard, some men hijacked the boat and brought him and the asshole's daughter with them. Cartel, obviously. Probably Diego Santiago. He'd pull something like this. No idea why, though."

Ignacio didn't need to hear any more. He'd seen Diego on the street a few times. Everyone was scared of him. He walked like sharks swam. But Ignacio knew where the man was. You don't get to be the leader of the street rats without knowing where every important person lived.

And you don't get to kidnap my aunt without paying a big price. The price of the streets, he thought.

It was time to gather the crew and see who was up to show what they were really made of.

THIRTEEN

Ernie felt like he didn't really know his daughter, and wanted to take the time to talk to her privately and see where she was coming from.

He also knew that nothing said in this villa, no matter where they sat, was going to be truly private. He was sure Diego had cameras and microphones everywhere, even in their bathrooms.

"How did Cuba treat you?" Ernie figured he'd start this conversation out easy, making small talk. "Nice weather today, too."

Grace smiled faintly. "I give you credit, Ernie. You did something I never thought I'd see you do."

Ernie smiled back. "And what's that?"

"Fool someone." Grace stood and walked over to the alcohol cabinet and poured herself some scotch. She went to the window and stared out. "This is all so tiring, don't you think?"

Ernie wanted to get up and wrap his arms around his daughter but her body language told him that was a bad idea. "Can you pour me a drink, too?"

Grace waved her glass at the cabinet. "Help yourself. I don't work for you. I never have and I never will."

Ernie hoped she was just in a bad mood today or maybe it was her time of the month. "I'll get it myself. Not a big deal."

As soon as he rose and moved toward the alcohol, Grace circled away from him and sat back down.

"I do wonder whether or not you can actually see this thing through to the end," Grace said. "For instance: when Diego decides he no longer needs you, and that will definitely happen soon, will you be able to stop him from killing you, or will you lie down and help him put the gun in your mouth?"

Ernie shrugged as he poured his own drink. "Maybe that will never happen. Maybe Diego and I can come to a mutual understanding. This doesn't all magically end if we find treasure. Do you think I'll ever be happy? This isn't about the money, it's about the adventure. Even if I get my hands on the treasure, and it's all mine in the end... there are more sunken ships and buried treasure out there for me to find."

Grace shook her head. "I never understood you. If I had the money you had, I'd spend the rest of my life trying to spend it and be happy."

"Are you happy, though?" Ernie sat back down across from his daughter. "Truly happy?"

Grace didn't answer, looking into her glass.

"Money doesn't buy happiness. I don't really know what does, to be honest. I'm still trying to figure it out myself," Ernie said. "When I was growing up I was poor. Dirt poor. I started to make money, started to hustle and began a new life. Still, it took me a long time to realize I was happier when I was poor and didn't know any better. Does that make sense?"

"Nope." Grace put down her drink and folded her arms. "Poor people are stupid. That's why they're poor. I'll never be poor because I'm too smart." She sighed. "Too smart for my own good, I guess."

"Why do you say that?" Ernie finished his drink but didn't want to get up and refill his glass. Grace might actually say something personal, something important. He wondered when the last time they'd actually had a real, honest to goodness discussion. It had been many years.

Grace turned toward Ernie and at first he thought she was angry, but now he knew she was on the verge of tears. "I'm sick of all of this back and forth, cat and mouse stuff. Where's the damn treasure, Dad?"

Ernie sighed. Was Grace showing pure emotion, or was this another showing of her great acting skills? She could've been in movies or on TV, and if she'd wanted that he would've made sure it happened. But his daughter was too busy chasing the wrong boys and spending too much money to want to have to actually work.

"I wish I knew exactly where the treasure was, because at this point I'd trade it to Diego and the cartel for safe passage for both of us out of Mexico," Ernie said.

Grace shook her head. "No. Not the answer I was looking for, on either count."

"What do you mean?"

"I want the treasure. For me. For us. After all of this back and forth, after all of the dives and the double-crosses and being held as a prisoner... I deserve to walk away from Mexico with my head held high, and my suitcases stuffed with diamonds and gold," Grace said.

Ernie knew her supposed tears had been an act. He felt responsible for it, too. How many nights had he argued with his wife about Grace, and how spoiled she was? He thought he was doing good for his daughter by giving in to her every demand, by her not wanting for anything and making it hard for her to have it.

Instead, he'd raised a monster. A sociopath. His wife had always told Ernie she was scared of her own daughter, which got him so upset and frustrated.

But she'd been right. All this time, Grace had been manipulating everyone around her. Pulling the strings like a damn puppet master.

"We follow along with what Diego wants, and in the end we'll find the treasure," Grace said. She'd gotten up and refilled her glass. "Do whatever we need to do to stay in his good graces, and then see if he believes we're entitled to a portion of the treasure."

"And if he doesn't?" Ernie asked.

Grace shrugged and turned toward her father. She took a sip of her drink before running her thumb from her free hand across her throat.

Ernie shook his head. To kill Diego would take skill he knew he didn't have, but it would also be an open war against the biggest cartel in the world. Hundreds, if not thousands, of sicarios, would have an open contract for them.

"We'd never survive," Ernie said quietly. If Diego had cameras in the room he'd clearly see the motion Grace had just done. The doors might bust open any second and they'd both be dead.

Grace groaned. "I'm just venting. That's all." She turned slowly in a circle and waved her hand. "Hey, Diego... I'm getting frustrated and sick of all of this. Find the damn treasure already and let us go, or just let us go now. You're probably never going to find it. We've likely been looking in the wrong area completely. What if the treasure is off the coast of Peru or Australia?"

Ernie came up to Grace. "You need to be careful. Don't antagonize him. He holds our life in his hands right now."

Grace stared at Ernie with open contempt in her eyes. "I will not back down to a murderer. To a man who shows no respect for women, either. Do you honestly think Diego is going to let us live if we find the treasure or we never do? Not a chance. He'll use us to help him until it's found or he gives up. Guess what? That's the point where his men put a bullet in the back of your head. Mine, too. Even if I give in and sleep with him. I'm still going to die."

"Sleep with him? What?" Ernie couldn't believe what he was hearing.

Grace nodded. "He's already made his first pass at me, and it wasn't with a handful of roses. Diego Santiago is going to get his way with me, whether I like it or not."

Ernie felt the anger rise inside of him. He wanted to stay in control and see this through to the end, hoping a situation would happen that he could escape and take his daughter with him.

Diego had made it perfectly clear to Ernie that he needed to step up and be a good father and take care to protect his only child.

FOURTEEN

Two against one. She'd been in worse situations.

JoJo got ready while Cuba and Alberto waited for her in the kitchen. They'd stopped talking when they saw she was up, but she'd heard enough to know that Alberto could no longer be trusted.

If Cuba believed Alberto, then she was screwed. Her time here wouldn't last much longer. JoJo wasn't sure if Cuba would actually kill her, but letting her go when she would run to the same people who were going to try to take him down didn't seem like an option he would entertain.

She sat quietly as the boat drove out to the next dive spot. None of them really said much on the way. It seemed like everyone was thinking about the same thing – this new issue with the cartel. Cuba was probably building a plan in his head about how to get out of this situation. Alberto had shown his cards in the morning when he chose Cuba over her.

JoJo had no choice at the moment but to continue doing what she had been doing since she'd gotten herself involved in this whole treasure mess.

Alberto made a sharp turn and cut the engine.

"We're here," he said, glancing at her with guilty eyes.

JoJo looked over the side of the boat as the churning water stilled. The water was still fairly clear in this area, and she could vaguely discern the ocean floor.

"There's nothing here," she said, and leaned back in her seat.

"We dive," Cuba responded, pulling the zipper up the back of his suit.

"Don't be an idiot. Look at the water. Nothing is down there. Let's move on instead of wasting our time."

JoJo didn't know if she should be pushing Cuba's buttons at this point, considering her precarious situation, but she just wasn't in the mood for bullshit today.

"Under the sand. Just because you can't see it, doesn't mean it's not down there."

"No, it just means we have to waste another day sifting. Come on, even you have to admit this is getting ridiculous at this point. The better way to spend our time would be to get out of the water and try to find some kind of clue as to where it must be. Go check out historical nautical books or something."

"I was never one for reading. Do you know what gets you rich in this world? Hard work, perseverance, and taking advantage of those who are weaker than you."

JoJo thought she heard the last part directed at her, but Cuba gave her a wink, spit in his mask and dunked it into the water to wash it out.

She didn't really have a choice in her current situation. She'd been getting bolder at speaking her mind, but when it came down to it Cuba still had the upper hand. Even with Rick gone and working with the cartel, or at least for someone rogue within the cartel.

Alberto helped her with the airline. In this shallow of water, there was no point using tanks. Breathing treated air was a waste and a strain on their bodies.

Cuba dropped into the water and JoJo was about to follow when Alberto grabbed her.

"Don't believe everything you hear. He needs to trust somebody, right? That's all I was doing. Giving him someone to trust when he found out about you hiding info about the whole cartel thing."

"He found that out from you."

Alberto shook his head. "He would have found it out sooner than later. It was better if it came from me. Another level of trust. Now, he'll make sure to keep a harder eye on you, and I can get away with a lot more."

"Why should I believe you?"

"You only have two lifelines right now. This," Alberto shook the air line, "and me."

Before she could reply, he pushed her into the water.

The water spun around her for a moment before she was able to gather her surroundings. Cuba was kneeling at the bottom, having already brought the vacuum with him. He motioned for her to get down there.

At least he was considerate enough to wait so she didn't have to swim down into a cloud of sand and silt.

They worked for a couple hours, moving across the ocean floor trying to reveal something of interest, before going back to the surface for a break.

"I told you there's nothing down there. Either move on or call it a day," JoJo said.

Cuba grunted and waved her off, flinging his gloves across the boat. She didn't know him well enough to know if this reaction was good for her or bad.

Some people thrive when they get frustrated, and the more pissed off they get, the more it seems to help them. While other people wind up getting so flustered that they can't do the simplest thing and spiral out of control. Some get violent.

Cuba, based on his actions since their unfortunate meeting, was most likely the latter.

JoJo looked into the distance.

"Hey, look at that. Isn't that your place?" She asked Cuba. "We should have just started searching from here. Ruled out this area earlier on. Clearer water, easier to dive. It's a no brainer to get this out of the way first. But I guess you need brains for that."

She was pushing it, but needed to see how he would react.

"Get our stuff from the bottom and let's get out of here. Before you become a buried treasure, bitch."

Good, JoJo thought. *Get him pissed and he seemed to give in to giving up easier.*

She was at the bottom, gathering what they'd left, when something reflected off the surface above.

She stopped what she was doing and looked into the distance. A moment later, another glint came from the surface and flashed in the water. It wasn't something above, like a boat, a surfer, or something else. This was coming from under the water and reflecting off the ripples and back down. The area was shallow enough to allow the sun's rays to penetrate far enough down.

JoJo looked above her. The boat was swaying gently, but nobody was watching her. Most likely, Cuba was fuming and lost in his head.

JoJo disconnected her air line and swam as best as she could toward whatever object was in the water. She wasn't worried about running out of breath since she was still in good shape and could hold her breath long enough to get to the surface if she didn't make it all the way there.

She was almost to the object when she heard the boat's engine roar to life and head her way. She cursed and took one last look before heading to the surface. There was definitely something there. It looked like a piece of formed metal, like a door hinge.

Or the corner of a treasure chest, she thought.

The boat was almost on her when she surfaced.

"What the hell do you think you're doing?" Cuba said, his face red and eyes crazy.

"I saw a shadow heading toward me. Thought it was a shark. I panicked."

"Well get the hell on the boat then instead of waiting to have your legs bitten off. We still have work to do and I need all of you."

JoJo climbed on the boat and spun around, estimating where the object was in reference to Cuba's abandoned house. When the time was right she would have to come back here.

Alone.

FIFTEEN

The men had come silently in the middle of the day, in front of everyone on the street. No one looked twice as Ignacio and his mother were taken away.

They'd entered the apartment quickly and efficiently, going room to room, weapons drawn.

Not a word as they pointed the guns at Ignacio and his mother, slipped bags over their heads, and escorted them down the stairs to a waiting SUV.

No one on the street said a word, no one ran off to get the police.

In seconds, the SUV was gone and the street went back to its normal life.

"Where are you taking us?" Ignacio prayed they would be safe, and knew this was all because of him. His mother didn't deserve to be involved. She had done nothing wrong.

"Shhh. Soon," was the only answer he got despite his many questions. Within a half an hour or so, they arrived at their destination.

Ignacio and his mother were led across pavement and then brickwork driveways and into a building with fans blowing.

When the hoods were pulled from their heads, Ignacio blinked a few times. Confused.

"Aunt Maria?"

His aunt ran to Ignacio and gave him a big hug.

"I don't understand–"

"Say nothing. Everything is being recorded. Act dumb," Maria whispered to the boy. She pushed away from him and hugged her sister, giving her instructions as well.

"Come. It is lunchtime," Diego said from the doorway, waving his hand.

Maria led Ignacio by the hand and they all sat down at a large table, where burritos and tacos and various fruits were laid out.

"Eat, eat." Diego smiled at Ignacio's mother. "I am sorry for treating you so badly but I needed you to come with my men without any incidents. I'm sure you understand."

His mother glanced at Ignacio and then her sister before nodding slightly.

Ignacio was hungry and he filled his plate with food, heaping rice and beans onto his plate as well. He decided, if this was going to be his last meal, he might as well enjoy as much of it as possible.

"Why are we here?" His mother was addressing Diego but she kept looking at Maria.

"The boy," Diego said. "I need his help, and I also need to keep him safe."

Ignacio had bitten into a taco but at the words of Diego he nearly choked on the food.

Keep me safe? Why? Who is coming after me? Does he know about the treasure? I might need to figure out an escape route, Ignacio thought.

He took another bite and tried not to make eye contact with Diego, afraid of what he might see in the evil man's eyes.

"Ignacio's crew will be helpful to us, but there are outside forces looking for him," Maria said. She stared at Ignacio. "You are officially retired from this game. You will be sidelined but help in another role. Do you understand?"

"No, I do not." Ignacio dropped the rest of his taco back onto his plate. "They are my crew. If you need their help, then I need to lead them."

"Impossible. I will not let my… you stay involved. There is a vast treasure out there, somewhere, and we need to find it without issues. You will be protected," Diego said.

"I can handle myself." Ignacio sighed. Now what could he do? If he was being guarded all day and night, he'd never be able to get out of the villa and back to the treasure.

"You have the full run of the property but you will not be able to go back into town." Maria smiled at Ignacio. "I know this doesn't seem fair to you, but this is the only way to keep my family safe."

"I can handle myself," Ignacio said again. He looked at Diego. "Where is Rick?"

Diego smiled. "He is here. Upstairs right now. I asked Rick and his cohorts to give us through lunch to talk with you. Let you know the rules now. Maybe you and Rick can go swimming this afternoon."

"I don't have a bathing suit," Ignacio said.

"I bought you a couple of different ones to try. Don't worry. You will be taken care of." Maria reached over and squeezed his hand. "Now eat, before your food gets cold."

Ignacio decided to put his head back down and eat. Figure out exactly what was happening, what he could do, and when he could start to do it.

I'll need Rick's help first, he thought. If he could find a spot where they could talk, maybe he could get Rick to help get the treasure out of the ocean and hidden away for them.

Ignacio also worried about Catalina, since he knew it had been a mistake to let her know where it was. By now, she might have already let the crew know about it, or maybe an adult in her family. The gold could be long gone.

They finished lunch in silence, everyone taking turns glancing at everyone else at the table.

Ignacio made sure he ate as much as he could fit in his stomach and then an extra burrito. He hoped the rumor of not swimming after you'd eaten wasn't true, because he figured the only safe place to talk with Rick would be swimming in the pool.

"Maria, show them to their rooms. I'll get Rick and tell him Ignacio is here," Diego said. He smiled. "Or, as he likes to call you, Nacho."

Ignacio groaned. "I do not like being called that."

"And I do not blame you." Diego put an arm around Ignacio's shoulder but then pulled back, looking suddenly uncomfortable. "Go and see what Maria has bought for you."

Ignacio followed Maria and his mother upstairs and down the hallway, past closed bedroom doors.

"There are two bedrooms with an adjoining door," Maria said. She glanced at her sister. "I am so sorry to get you involved in this, but it was the only way to keep you safe. There is a group of people that are after something, and they will stop at nothing to find it."

Ignacio knew Maria was talking about Cuba and his team, or what was left of them. He assumed the cartel wasn't directly behind Diego, either, so there could be many factions at play. It would be good to keep an open mind and open eyes at all times. There was no telling who was the enemy and who was the friend, and it seemed to Igancio that those relationships were changing rapidly.

He tried on the swimming trunks and smiled. He'd talk to Rick and see what he knew. If anything had been found out since they'd last met.

Diego would be watching them, trying to get them to slip up and openly talk about what they knew.

Ignacio wondered if Diego was smart enough to know Ignacio knew a lot more than he'd led on, and worried about the treasure and whose hands it might end up in.

It needs to be in my hands and anyone who is loyal to me, Igancio thought.

SIXTEEN

Ernie pushed Baker away from the door. It wasn't easy. Ernie had more mass on him, but when Baker got moving it was like trying to stop a bear.

"I don't care what Diego said. Do you smell that food?" Baker whined, rubbing the spot on his chest where Ernie had checked him.

"Of course I do, and I don't like that guy anymore than you do. But for now, we appease him and stay in here until he's done talking with the kid."

"It's bullshit. The whole time here we get crap thrown together at the last minute. Now the kid's here and first thing is a table full of delicious food. We should be the ones getting pampered. What's the boy going to do?"

"You mean the boy who got shot and bounced back? The kid who has been running the town's street rats with no competition? The one who obviously is somehow connected to Diego more than we know?"

"Yeah, that one," Baker said, sounding less sure of his argument.

"Exactly, now calm down. We'll get food once they're done with whatever this is."

Ernie switched channels on the television. More soap operas. In Spanish. He wasn't sure if it was better when you could understand these stupid shows, or when you caught a word or two here and there.

He turned it off and looked out the window overlooking the pool. He wasn't going to let Baker know, but he was probably the most hungry out of the two. Sure, beans and rice, tortillas and cheese were delicious, but they didn't help him in the bathroom department. Ernie figured he got rid of the food just as fast as he got it down. Probably wasn't absorbing the little nutrition into his system.

He needed something solid. Steak and potatoes. A burger. Pizza. What wouldn't he give for a pizza right now?

Ernie turned to Baker.

"What?" Baker asked.

"I understand why I should be getting pampered. None of this treasure crap would be going on if it wasn't for me. But what are you contributing here?"

"What's that supposed to mean? I'm a government agent. I have connections. I have... I, um."

"You don't really have much to offer, Baker. You're rogue. Nobody in your alphabet agency is going to help you. In fact, it seems like they may have sent that crazy-ass See guy to take care of you. You know why you're still here? Because you're with me."

Baker seemed to take in what he was saying and began to look very nervous as the truth settled in. The guy was a loose end. Not exactly dangerous, but not much more than a hanger-on. Ernie had grown to like him, as much as he could like anyone on that side of the law. But he wondered how much being under his umbrella could protect him.

"We'll figure it out. Don't worry about it for now," Ernie said, trying to calm him down.

"I shouldn't have to worry about it at all, but here I am. I've helped everyone out, and now I'm suddenly the outsider? Do you know how many times I could have had the DEA swarm the entire area? I'm not looking for a bust, I'm looking for a better life."

"Seriously, calm it down. I shouldn't have even said anything. Hell, I'm probably the only one who even thought of it. They know you're with me, and as long as that is the case you'll be fine."

"You sure?"

"Of course I'm sure."

Ernie wasn't sure.

He wondered how much pull he had with the cartel. How much influence. Whether they would listen to anything he had to say, or were just going to use him and then toss his dead body overboard. The cartel wasn't known for letting many outsiders stay alive for longer than they were useful.

Someone knocked on the door. Baker jumped. Ernie cursed inwardly. Now the guy was never going to act the same. Just having some conversation and he had to say something stupid. Ernie was good at what he did, but he never learned when to keep his mouth shut.

The door opened and Rick poked his head through.

"Family time is over. Let's get some food and sit by the pool."

Maria and Diego were already outside by the time the three of them made it downstairs. Ernie eyed the table, filled with its usual food assortment, none of the delicious smells that had been tempting him while he was forced to stay in the room.

"Damn tacos. Never thought I'd get tired of tacos, but for the love of God can I have a burger?" Baker said to himself.

They all grabbed some food anyway. It may have been the same-old-same-old, but it was still delicious meat and cheese in a tortilla.

Diego waved them over when they walked out to the patio.

"We all have to talk. Some news has come up that changes things a bit."

Diego was about to say something else when a high-pitched scream came from out of sight. Ernie watched as a shirtless Nacho came around the corner, running, and leaped into the pool. He saw the scar from the bullet wound and was reminded that the kid should have been dead. But here he was, somehow back in their lives.

"Mr. Rick, come swimming. Look – no sharks." Ignacio spun around in the pool.

"In a bit, Nacho. I'm eating. Have to wait half an hour before swimming. Or is it an hour?" Rick asked Ernie.

"How would I know? I eat in the pool."

Diego explained the situation to them. Nacho apparently knew where the treasure was. Ernie wasn't sure if the kid was playing the guy, or if he'd actually found something. He couldn't keep the shocked look off of his face. The only person who didn't seem caught by surprise was Rick. Ernie would have to file that away for later.

"So the issue is, what am I supposed to do with all of you now?" Diego asked. "I brought you here to help find it. Now I have an answer, or at least the person who has the answer. Now I have three men, and a bitchy young woman staying at my place who offers me nothing of value."

"We can get you Cuba," Ernie said.

Diego waved his hand. "My men can get me that bastard. My dilemma is whether to part ways, let you all go and pretend like nothing happened, or... another option."

"We're all on the same side here," Ernie said, noticing Baker stiffening. "We can still be of use. Do the things you don't want your bosses knowing you're behind."

"You have a point with that, I guess. But what about him?" Diego pointed at Baker. "He appeared to be a valuable asset at first, but now that I'm thinking about it, what has he actually done? I mean–"

"Wait," Ernie said, holding up his hand. Not the smartest gesture to make to a made cartel man. "Speaking of bitchy young woman, where's Grace?"

Everybody at the table went silent and looked around. Diego motioned for a couple of his guards to go find her in the house.

As much as Ernie didn't want his daughter involved with this, he prayed she was in the house somewhere. If Grace had somehow managed to slip by Diego's men and take off, they were going to have much bigger problems than having to convince him that they were still useful.

In his heart, Ernie already knew that the house was empty.

SEVENTEEN

Catalina wondered if she was doing the right thing.

I'm doing the right thing for my family, for my people, for everyone I care about, she thought.

Arturo and three of the other boys were smiling because they knew they were about to be rich.

"We need to do this quickly and quietly, understand?" Catalina stared at the four and waited for each of them to nod in turn. "There is going to be a definite plan we all have to follow. Don't overthink it and don't do anything I don't tell you to do. Otherwise we'll have not only the cartel but everyone in town after us."

"Let's go get this treasure already," Arturo asked.

Catalina smiled. The boy was always so impatient, and he was always going to be no matter how many more years of life he had left in him.

"Did you get the items I asked for?" Catalina knew they needed a few things that they could easily carry through town without too many eyes following them. Just a bunch of kids doing whatever kids did.

The wheelbarrow filled with two-by-fours, shovels, a pickaxe and tarps might mean they were heading into the woods to make a tree fort. Children loved to do things like that, right?

Once they got to the beach, Catalina was glad to see the other three wheelbarrows had already been stashed behind some Mexican bush sage, along with the tools.

It would be a long walk through the center of town once they had the treasure, and if anyone looked under the tarps they'd be caught.

Catalina had thought it might be smarter to do this at night, but she knew the sounds of chopping into the wooden chests would attract unwanted attention. Her hope was by doing it in the daytime no one would bother to see what was happening, and even if they took a look they'd see a bunch of kids playing on the beach.

"There are a few chests, filled with treasure," Catalina said. "Our goal is simple: we crack them open and empty them out. Fill the wheelbarrows with all of it and then head to the warehouse I've secured for us."

She knew no one would bother them once they got to the warehouse, because it was supposedly haunted. On the outskirts of town. Where dark rituals had once been performed, if you could believe the urban legend.

Catalina didn't believe in ghosts or demons. She believed in herself and in getting rich.

Arturo was right behind her as she took a pickaxe and waded into the water. The tide would rise soon enough, so they needed to work quickly.

"Bring the wheelbarrows as close to the water as you can," Catalina said to the other three boys. "Empty them out but keep the items nearby."

"Let me do it," Arturo said to Catalina as she hefted the pickaxe. "I'm stronger."

Catalina shrugged and handed it over to Arturo, who was smiling at the submerged chest in front of them.

He took an overhead swing, slamming the pickaxe into the top of the chest.

"Be careful. We don't want to damage any of it," Catalina said.

Arturo swung several times, only making a small dent in the wood.

"My turn," Catalina said. She saw the other three boys watching intently from the shore and wondered if they could be trusted. Maybe she'd made a mistake involving so many others, but she needed to get the treasure moved before Ignacio came back for it.

Ignacio. I am so sorry, but this is what has to be. Life is not fair, Catalina thought.

There was a part of her that felt guilty for stealing it out from under Ignacio, but she knew he was never going to be able to share it with anyone. The cartel had their hooks in him, and he always did the right thing to protect his family.

Ignacio would hand it over, every last piece, in order to secure his freedom for his mother and aunt. This would all go to waste, and the cartel would get richer off of it. Make their lives a living hell in this town and every other town and village in Mexico.

She drove the pickaxe into the wood, splintering it. Creating a hole that was quickly filled with water as the waves crashed over the chest.

"There are a few of them here," Arturo said. He turned to the three boys. "Bring me another ax. Hurry."

While Arturo waited for another tool, Catalina attacked the hole in the chest and widened it slowly. She couldn't see inside because water kept rushing in as quickly as she brought the pickaxe up over her head for another blow.

Catalina smiled when the wood split and she grabbed it with her bare hands and pulled a chunk off it off of the top of the chest.

"What do you see?" Arturo asked.

Catalina grinned. "Our future. We need to hurry. It will be high tide soon. If we can get the top two chests emptied quickly, we might be able to cover the ones on the bottom and come back at low tide. Hurry."

She made the hole bigger and was glad to see Arturo was making progress in the next chest. With any luck they'd have this all done in the next day or two.

"I broke through," Arturo said and laughed. "We are rich."

Catalina nodded, even though she knew they weren't all going to be rich. As soon as the treasure was secured, she'd need to make a few drastic but needed decisions. "You told no one else, right?"

Arturo smiled. "I'm not stupid. Of course not."

Catalina turned to the other three. "How about you? Did you tell anyone what we found or what we were doing today?"

All three shook their heads.

"Good. Keep it that way. This will be a nice surprise for friends and family... once we secure it all and make sure no one is coming after us," Catalina said. "If word gets out we have this... we will all die a long and horrible death."

She turned and went back to work on the chest.

Arturo made a decent hole in his and shoved his hands inside, pulling out a golden lamp. "Ha. A genie is inside, right? I can make a wish."

Catalina snatched it from him. "Don't be stupid. If it really is a genie lamp, you'll waste a wish and people might be able to see the genie if it is big enough. Use your head." She turned and waved for the three boys to begin collecting the loot and filling the wheelbarrows.

Inside the chest she'd broken into she saw gold coins, maybe thousands. Strings of pearls and shiny rings and necklaces.

I am rich. I am very, very rich, Catalina thought.

EIGHTEEN

If I was smart, I'd leave. And I am smart, so why haven't I left? Grace thought as she made her way back to Cuba's wrecked house.

It had been surprisingly easy to sneak out of Diego's property. So easy that she probably could have just waltzed out waving goodbye at everyone. He must have gotten so complacent with them, thinking they were so happy to be out from under Cuba's fist that nobody had any desire to leave.

Granted, she wasn't sure if they ever were actual hostages, but when dealing with the cartel you were almost never just welcome guests.

Once Grace overheard that the kid knew where the treasure was, she figured they were all screwed one way or another. And how the hell had the kid known where the treasure was? And for how long?

A few insights came to Grace before she decided to leave everyone behind. The kid was no diver. He could barely swim. So wherever the treasure was, it had to be somewhere in shallow water. The problem with that is that the shallow areas changed with the tides. It would be just as much of a pain to find it as it was diving random spots around the original map area.

There were a couple of possibilities that she could pursue. The kid ran a street gang. What was the probability that he confided to someone else in the gang as to the location of the treasure? Grace knew how she was at that age. Spilling the tea about any spicy situation was almost required among her and her friends. Could she find one of them and trick the location out?

Something else was bothering her, also and, if it was true, she had screwed herself by leaving Diego's place. Rick was very close to the kid. Grace wasn't sure how close, but it was possible that maybe he knew about it. Before Cuba's place was raided, Rick had been going out a lot on his own. He never mentioned what he did, and nobody asked because he was quickly becoming seen as a lame duck, only kept around because of Cuba's obsession with JoJo.

If Rick knew, would he talk? Grace didn't think it mattered anymore. If the kid had agreed to show Diego where it was, Rick's information would be redundant. Relegated to a lame duck once more.

Grace rounded the bend where the wreck of Cuba's house, her former prison, came into view. Parts of it were still smoking, though it looked like the east wing had been put out in time to save more of the structure. She was hoping that was the case. The east wing was where the bedrooms were at.

A group of kids with wheelbarrows ran past her, one of them almost clipping her side. Grace cursed at them and one yelled a quick apology back to her as they continued doing whatever stupid kids do to keep themselves occupied.

She picked her way through the parts of rubble that looked the safest, having to move some large pieces in order to get through to the part of the house that was still standing.

The walls were scorched and there were some holes in the wall from where fire punched through, but for the most part it looked the same as when they had all been kept there. A more silent, creepy kind of the same.

Only as she got closer to her room did she hear a sound. Something rustled in one of the other rooms. Probably a lizard or some birds picking at the ruins. However, as far as she was aware neither of those animals knew how to swear or slam drawers.

Grace crept forward toward the open door the stranger was in. Could it be someone sent from the cartel to go through the place for clues? Scavengers from town looting the place for valuables? Either way, she needed to be careful. The smart thing to do would be to just leave and wait to see who came out, but she was never one to take the safe route.

Grace peeked around the door jamb and saw the back of someone bent over and throwing things out of the nightstand, still cursing.

"Nice ass," Grace said as she entered the room.

JoJo screamed and jumped back, knocking the lamp off the nightstand.

"Jesus Christ, Grace, are you trying to kill me?"

"If I wanted to do that, I could have done it plenty of times."

"What are you doing here?"

"I need something I left. Looks like you're doing the same."

JoJo sighed and held up her left hand. "Rick gave me a ring a while ago. I guess you can say we were engaged, but that was so many years ago it's almost as if it never happened. I took it off after the whole drug thing. Mostly just to make him sweat. Never put it back on and then this place gets trashed and it looks like the ring is gone for good. I checked everywhere."

"Give me a second," Grace said.

She went into her room and had her own mini-freak-out until she saw her earrings on the floor by the bed. She'd have to get in contact with Ernie and this was the only way to do it since she probably wasn't welcome back to Diego's.

"Speaking of Rick, I have to ask you something," Grace said when she walked back into JoJo's room. "How well did he know that Nacho kid?"

Grace got on her knees by the bed and reached her arm underneath it.

"As good as a grown adult can know a child, I guess. Why? And what are you doing?"

"Well enough for the kid to confide something big with him?"

"Probably. Nacho seemed to think Rick was some American bad-ass. Plus no father figure, so he put Rick in that role. The kid's a little shit, but he adores Rick."

Grace got to her feet and held out the ring to JoJo.

"Whenever you can't find something, it's always under the bed. Nacho knows where the treasure is. He hasn't said anything to Diego yet, as far as I know, but I'm sure he's said something to someone. His crew. Rick. Both."

"If he told someone, it would be Rick. His crew are a bunch of backstabbing crotch rockets. He wouldn't be dumb enough to say something to them. I just saw a handful of them when I got here. Out on the beach arguing."

"Wheelbarrows? They tried to run me over when I was walking up. Little shits."

Grace and JoJo chuckled before stopping and staring at each other. Without saying a word, they both ran out of the house, across the street, and to the beach.

"Follow the wheel marks."

"I am."

They got down to just above the waterline, where the trail ended.

"During the last dive, I saw a chest in the water, close by here. But it was too deep for them to do anything about it without diving equipment. And there's no way, even if they did get to it, that they'd be able to drag the thing back to shore."

"Tide changes. Could be there's a significant change in levels around here. Besides what else would they be doing? Nacho must have said something."

"Yeah, he did," JoJo said as she picked a coin off the sand. "This is definitely not a peso."

NINETEEN

There's so much more work to be done, Catalina thought. They'd only been able to break into three of the chest and only gotten the contents of the first two into the wheelbarrows and to the warehouse.

"Are we going back now?" Arturo asked.

They'd deposited the treasure into a handful of plastic tubs that had been left in the warehouse. Most of them were cracked but they still held the contents.

And what contents they were.

Catalina had never seen so many riches, not even in a museum or on television.

There were thousands of gold and silver coins, all loose. Bracelets and brooches and necklaces and rings. Silverware made of gold, rubies the size of her fist, and even a couple of crowns.

Worth millions of dollars, Catalina thought. *Enough for all of us already, and there could be another dozen chests still to open.*

"No. We wait." Catalina had already set up a desk and chair in the corner, and now she sat down and put her feet up on the dusty desk. "If we're seen running around with wheelbarrows so soon, someone might get suspicious. Too many people already saw us."

The boys with them began scooping up gold coins and putting them in their pockets.

Catalina opened the top drawer of the desk and sat up. "Wait... what do you think you're doing?"

One of the boys grinned. "We're rich. I'm going to buy food for my family."

"I'm going to buy them a new house," another boy said.

"No. Absolutely not. We can't spend any of this money, you idiots. This isn't a handful of pesos a street kid might happen upon or take from a tourist's pocket. If anyone sees even one of these coins they'll know there are more of them. They'll ask you where you got it, and force you to tell them."

The boys looked either confused or unconcerned, caught up in the excitement of the find.

Catalina turned to Arturo. "And you?"

"What about me?"

"Do you plan on ruining this by taking coins, too? Are you that short-sighted and greedy, like they are?" Catalina asked.

"No. I say we leave it all until we get the rest. Then we figure out a sensible way to split it all, so no one gets hurt," Arturo said.

Catalina was staring at Arturo. "Can I trust you?"

"Of course."

"Then stand back." Catalina stood, drawing the Glock from the desk drawer. She'd taken it from one of her uncles a few weeks ago, thinking at some point she might need it. As she'd gotten older, more and more creepy men had been looking too long at her as she passed by, and she knew it was only a matter of time before one of them made his move.

She had the Glock nearby on most occasions, and had stashed it here when she'd taken over the warehouse.

Now she pointed at the three boys. "I need you to empty your pockets. Right now. Put it all back. There will be plenty of time to take your fair share."

All three boys began emptying their pockets, watching Catalina as she moved toward them, weapon drawn.

"Do you really trust me, Arturo?" Catalina asked.

"I do, I do." He didn't look scared, more curious as he watched her walk past him and to the boys and the treasure.

"Then this will only help us," Catalina said. She shot all three boys before they could react, not expecting her to actually kill them. Not one of them even had a chance to turn away or begin to run.

Arturo sighed.

Catalina turned toward him, but lowered the Glock. "We'll need to figure out how to get the rest of the treasure on our own."

"You should have let them go with a warning, and then they could do all the heavy lifting," Arturo said.

"Too risky. They would come back tonight and try to take some of it." Catalina shook her head. "No, now we have to do it ourselves. Are you physically up to the challenge?"

"I am. I am still hurting but I can manage, especially for all of this."

Catalina smiled. "All of this and so much more. As soon as night falls we will head back with two wheelbarrows and work through the night if we must."

"What if we're spotted?"

"We're just a couple of dumb street kids racing wheelbarrows in the street. No big deal, right? As long as we act like we're having fun and not doing anything important, we might get away with it. After midnight, when only the bad people are out, will be the challenge for us," Catalina said.

Arturo went over to the plastic tubs, stepping over the dead children. "We have so much now, already. What if this is more than enough for both of us?"

"It might never be enough. If anyone finds the chests for the rest of it, they'll see two are empty. They'll come looking for them. Maybe tear the town apart looking." Catalina shook her head again. "We're in this too deep now. We see it to the end. There is nothing else to do but retrieve the rest and smash the chests apart and let the tide take the pieces away."

Arturo shrugged. "Then I suggest we go home and get some sleep. We have a long night ahead of us."

Catalina went and sat back down in the chair and put the Glock in the drawer but didn't close it. "I'm not going anywhere. Not until it's time to get some more of the treasure."

"Does anyone else know about this?" Arturo asked. He walked over and sat on the edge of the desk.

"Only Ignacio and the two of us, as far as I know."

Arturo snorted. "Can he be trusted?"

Catalina laughed. "Obviously far more than you and I can be trusted. We stole this right out from under his nose. He'll never forgive either of us, but I have something you don't possess."

Arturo stared at her.

"He is in love with me, the same as you are. I can bend your will with ease because growing boys are stupid and turn into stupid men," Catalina said. "He will, in time, forgive me."

"Ignacio will want to kill me. He's wanted to do it before this happened, so this will only give him more incentive." Arturo sighed again. "Maybe we should take what we have and run. Start a new, better life."

Catalina put her hand in the drawer but didn't pull out the Glock. "No. We do as planned and we both get more treasure and then we begin new lives."

Arturo slowly nodded his head and stared at the three dead boys on the floor.

Catalina knew she should have waited to kill them, but they weren't going to do as she said anymore. She worried Arturo would do the same.

"Stay here with me until it's time to go," Catalina said.

She worried Arturo would leave and head straight for the chests, taking whatever he could carry and disappearing. Worse, he might enlist a few more from the crew to help him.

Catalina knew what she had to do. Once all of the treasure was secured, she'd figure out the best way to use it to her advantage. Maybe then she could tell Ignacio, and paint a picture as if she did it for the both of them.

He might be able to dispose of it, turn it into actual cash, which they could spend.

Which she could spend, because her ultimate goal was to have it all to herself.

TWENTY

The first thing Ernie did was excuse himself and go to his room.

Grace may have been gone – Diego's men found no trace of her – but Ernie knew one way to find her. He just hoped she still had those earrings on. He tried to remember if he saw her with them since they'd gotten here.

Maybe she had taken them off, since there was no need to wear them when they were together, but took them with her when she escaped.

Unless she doesn't want you around, Ernie thought. *She could be out on her own planning to screw over everyone on every side.*

He pulled up the listening app on his phone and put it on speaker. He heard his daughter's voice immediately. Ernie quickly pressed the mute button. His initial plan was to open the app and try to talk to her, but she was with someone else. In Ernie's experience, nothing bad ever came from spying on someone's conversations. Even his daughter. Or Cuba's daughter.

Rick. Nacho. Nacho's street friends. Treasure.

He was understanding the words, but his brain was refusing to make sense out of it. At this point, they all knew the kid either found the treasure or thought he had. But the chance that he'd told Rick, who was sitting outside right now not saying anything, put a new spin on it.

They had a real issue now. Not just Ernie, but everyone else. He clicked off the app once he heard some kids had gotten away with the treasure. At this point, they were all just chasing nothing. Sure, some of them thought there was no treasure from the start, but this time there really wasn't.

Unless the street urchins hadn't taken all of it. It was possible. They were kids. How much could they salvage at one time? Only himself, Grace, and JoJo knew at this point they were fucked. It would need to stay that way for now.

Diego had basically said they were all useless at this point, since Nacho would lead him to the treasure. What if Ernie walked downstairs and declared he knew where it was. He'd bring them to it, and they'd find it already plundered. Certainly, Diego couldn't blame Ernie for that. Someone got to it before they did. It happened all the time in wreck recovery. It was a way out alive. At least, he hoped.

Then, once everything had settled down, he'd bring in some more of his men and they'd find these pain in the ass kids, take the treasure from them, maybe knock a few around to teach them a lesson, and leave the country with nobody knowing the difference.

Except Grace and JoJo. And since JoJo knew, that would mean Rick would find out also.

Would it be easier to give them a cut, or leave the estranged couple in a shallow ditch somewhere in the desert?

Ernie never shied away from killing if it was necessary. But he wasn't like Cuba, who thought it should be the first and only option whenever someone became a potential problem.

He wouldn't say he'd come to like the two of them. He'd had a problem with JoJo since it turned out she was only cozying up to him in order to get the map. But, since then, he'd grown a grudging respect for the two.

Both weren't above going beyond the law to get what they wanted, and seemed to get a kick out of doing it. His type of people. And Ernie wasn't delusional enough to think a woman as beautiful as JoJo would be after him for his looks. He'd always known it was some sort of money play. He had been fine with that. Had dealt with it many times before. The sex was worth the cost.

What really pissed him off was that they hadn't gotten to the sex part before she ran off with that useless map.

He decided he'd leave it up to Grace. She was wearing the earrings, so it meant that she hadn't completely abandoned him. That was his initial fear, though a part of him did wish she'd find a safe way out of Mexico and back to their oceanfront cliff house in Malibu.

He heard JoJo saying something about having to get back to Cuba before he started wondering where she was and sent someone after her. He waited a few more minutes while they said their goodbyes and was about to unmute the app and say something when Grace chimed in.

"Ernie, are you there?"

"Yes, I'm here. Why the hell did you leave? Leave, and not tell me you were going to?"

"Doesn't matter now. Did you hear anything that happened or did you just jump on?"

"I heard the important parts."

"Yeah, I figured you'd be listening in like some pervert. What do you think? I'm willing to work with JoJo, but I think it would be good for at least you to get the hell out of Diego's place and back over here. As much as it pains me to admit, you have more options available to you in this situation than I do."

"How much do you trust JoJo?"

"At the moment? She's the most trustworthy person I have. I'm sure as shit not going back to Cuba. He needs to be dealt with, also. If he finds out about these child pirates, that's game over."

"Let me think about this. Keep your earrings on. There may be a way for us to get Diego involved without him ultimately taking everything, and dealing with Cuba at the same time. I need to get Rick alone. That's going to be the difficult part now that Nacho is here and wants to play family time with him."

"What should I do in the meantime? There might be more treasure still there."

"Let the kids get it. Makes it easier on us. We don't have to deal with the recovery, and everything would be in one place, nice and neat. Go to the hotel suite we got when we came down here. I haven't checked out and the booking was made open-ended."

"I don't have the door card anymore."

"The desk will give it to you. If they don't remember you from when you had a hissy fit when your luggage wasn't brought to the room, just tell them Large Marge sent you."

"Excuse me?"

"You know how many times I lose things. It's the security word that lets them know it's okay to give you a new door card. No need to talk about it."

"Like in Pee Wee—"

"I said no need to talk about it. Just go there and lay low."

Ernie closed the app and put his phone down. There was nothing he could do, stuck here. He needed to keep playing the game for now. Come up with some plan to get Diego and Cuba to destroy each other, then get the treasure like he'd been planning to do since he flew down.

Whatever happened with Rick and JoJo, and even Baker, would play out on its own. What was important was getting himself and his daughter out of the country. Because, despite the facts, Grace was his daughter, and he'd always take care of her.

Cuba can die alone.

TWENTY-ONE

Cuba needed backup. More and more well-armed men to clear the town if need be. The cartel wanted a war? He was going to give it to them.

Never in his life had Cuba been burned this badly. He had lost key members of his team, had had his villa torched and all of his plans thrown aside.

The cartel has declared war on me, and that is not a good thing to do, Cuba thought.

He thought he still had JoJo by his side, although he couldn't remember the last time he'd seen her. Alberto, too? Maybe. He might have also left.

Cuba couldn't control anyone anymore.

He'd placed a call for an elite team to arrive in Mexico. Then called another. There was no way he could face the cartel might with only a handful of men, even if they were all killers.

Several dozen were needed, and since he'd long ago tapped into Ernie Patek's offshore bank accounts, money was no object.

They were going to arrive soon, at least the first wave of them, either via commercial flights or private jets. All armed to the teeth and ready to kill for the love of money.

Cuba took the bottle of rum and got a few steps before he realized it was nearly empty. He went back to the hotel bar and waved for the bartender to hand him two more.

"Don't you think you've had enough, sir?"

Cuba smiled. It was not pleasant. "Give me the fucking bottles or I will pull the hotel manager from his office and see that you are fired. I am an American citizen, which means I am better than you. I make more money in a week than you do in a year, so shut your mouth and give me what I asked for."

The bartender sighed and handed Cuba two bottles of rum before turning away.

Cuba stepped out and went to the far end of the pool area. He'd left the awful dwelling he'd been forced to go to, and was now several miles outside of the pitiful town.

When had this all fallen apart? This was supposed to be easy. Take the treasure, bond with his daughter, seduce JoJo and live his good life.

Instead, he was holed up in a boring hotel with a bunch of tourists who had no idea how close they were to cartel-controlled areas. No clue how easy it would be for them to be kidnapped and ransomed, or killed and strung up as a warning to others.

Cuba had done his research. Even the lethal gang, MS-13, steered clear of the area. The Sinaloa Cartel used them in various places in Mexico but not here. There wasn't enough action to keep the gang satisfied, and there were other cities and towns where their particular skills were needed.

He wondered what would happen if the cartel got their hands on the treasure. They would grow exponentially. Hire more killers, manufacture and distribute more drugs, pay off more people to look the other way.

Cuba knew they would control not only Mexico, not only South America, but the United States as well. With such vast wealth they would easily find those in America that had a hand out, regardless of what was about to flood the streets.

I'm doing this so it will not happen to my country, Cuba thought. He laughed as he finished the first bottle and opened one of the new ones. *Even I don't believe that garbage. I do it because I need to for my own personal growth, for my own personal wealth, and because... I fucking can.*

He finished half of the next bottle, feeling good, before he picked up his phone and began sending new messages for new teams to come to Mexico and do what was needed.

Since these militia recruits knew the danger, he'd promised them nearly double their salaries. He'd need a new villa, too, so he could house all of them. Hope there was no tension between each group.

Planes were arriving as he typed messages, and he coordinated for them to stay in a nearby, fancier hotel. They would come looking like tourists. In small groups of two and three. Weapons would be procured quickly as well as reliable transportation, bulletproof vests and any and all equipment they needed.

While it was tough to find rifles and pistols in Mexico, it wasn't out of the question. Cuba had already ordered a vast arsenal of weapons and ammo and knew it had arrived a couple of cities over, hidden within crates of imported olives.

I could eat some olives right now, Cuba thought. *With any luck they'd soak up all of this rum coursing through my veins. I need to stay focused.*

He wanted to call JoJo and see where she was, but he didn't have her number. Had he taken away her phone or had it been destroyed in the villa fire?

Cuba was staring at a little girl in the pool, swimming with her little brother. They looked so cute and innocent.

"What is your name, little one?" Cuba asked.

Right away her parents showed themselves, sitting up on their lounge chairs and looking scared.

Cuba waved at them and smiled. "I'm harmless. Just wanted to say hi. They look like they're having fun. Are you on vacation?"

The father stood and slowly walked toward Cuba, taking off his sunglasses. "Yes. Vacation. We don't want trouble from the locals."

"Locals? That is funny. I'm as American as you are, sir. By that accent I'd say you're hailing from Wisconsin or Minnesota."

"The latter." The man had stopped a few feet from Cuba, putting himself between Cuba and his children. "And you?"

"Puerto Rico. I've lived in Milwaukee. Philadelphia. Saratoga. Sayreville. Knoxville. Jacksonville." Cuba smiled. "Lots of places."

The mother was waving her children out of the pool.

Cuba looked over and saw one of the workers handing out drinks to another couple. Cuba loudly yelled for the man.

"Yes, sir?"

"This nice family is now my friends. I want them to have anything and everything they need while here on vacation. Do you understand?" Cuba took out a wad of cash from his pocket and peeled off several U.S. hundred dollar bills. "This should take care of it."

The father was waving. "No, sir, please... I don't need your money."

"But you want it. Everyone wants money," Cuba said. "This is a small gift from me to you and your lovely family. I scared your little ones and for that I am truly sorry."

"I cannot–"

Cuba stood with wobbly legs and picked up his rum bottles. "Enjoy your stay. I will not trouble you again." He turned toward the hotel worker. "Add this to their account, all of it. Then I want you to find me in the hotel and I will tip you generously. Have a fine day. I know I will."

He chuckled as he walked away.

Even in the face of certain death, with danger lurking around every corner, Cuba could still be a human being. He could still bring comfort and joy to civilians.

Cuba needed to take a quick nap and await the first arrivals, because he was going to bring death to the cartel and anyone that got in his way.

TWENTY-TWO

Baker took a plate full of tacos up to his room. Ernie had come back down and joined everyone outside, but Baker didn't want to deal with any of the same old conversations that were going on. He wanted to be alone with his food.

He really wanted to call his wife.

He'd avoided it because of not wanting to bring the agency down on him. But after Diego killed Agent See, he wasn't worried so much anymore. If the agency was planning to come after anyone, it would be Diego. Which was one reason why it wasn't good to stay here much longer.

Baker was bothered about what Ernie said earlier. Did everyone think he was useless? Dead weight? No, he wasn't. He refused to believe that.

Then he thought about his wife and how, even though it was unplanned, he'd basically abandoned her when everything started going downhill. It wasn't his fault. He had such high regard for his ability to work the field that it never crossed his mind that he would get dragged into the whole mess. He was supposed to sneak in and out, get the money, and leave with nobody knowing the difference other than the missing treasure.

Like he was Delta Force, or some James Bond type covert ops guy.

Stupid. Baker knew better. The fantasies of being out on the job and what he'd be able to do, all while sitting behind a desk getting more exercise from breathing than anything else, had become real in his head. He never realized just how much he had talked himself up to the point where he couldn't distinguish reality from his daydreams.

He was too scared to do it. To pick up that phone and hear his wife's ailing voice on the other end. To explain to her what he really was doing. What mess he was stuck in that he may not get out of.

It didn't matter that he started doing this for her. She wouldn't accept that as a reason. That was why he never told her the real reason he was going down to Mexico. She would have fought against it. He used to think she was too proud to take money that wasn't earned, no matter where it came from. Now, Baker was beginning to realize it had nothing to do with pride. She wouldn't have wanted him to go because she wanted him there with her. There would be no guarantee he'd make it back, without or without the riches, if he left.

And she was right. Here he was stuck in a cartel house, being told he was a loose end who contributed nothing. Maybe Ernie was right. He was crap at being a field agent, so why would he think he'd be any good negotiating his way through Mexican mafia, rogue gangsters, and fucking pirate treasure?

There was only one thing he could do: not only make himself useful, but make himself indispensable. But how?

Ernie had some kind of status around here, being a crook to begin with. Rick, though maybe not as connected as Ernie, could hold his own with the crowd. Hell, even Grace – wherever she was – had a tougher exterior than he did.

Baker was just a desk jockey, trained enough to get him a title and badge at the DEA, but not enough for defensive and counter-attack measures to become muscle memory.

He curled his arm and prodded at his bicep. It was there somewhere, under the weight he'd gained from four-thousand calorie lunches and the naps that followed.

But sometimes all somebody needed in order to get out of tricky situations alive was a reason strong enough to push their mind and body farther than expected. And Baker had that: his wife.

During this whole treasure hunt, with the dives, the bullets flying, running away from bad guys and then running back, he had lost track of the real goal. His reason for being here was not to get rich, but to try to get his wife the best palliative care possible.

People did a lot of stupid things for love, a lot of dangerous things. Nobody was above doing whatever it took to be with the person they loved, even if it was for just a little while longer. Was it selfish? Sure, but love doesn't just make you blind, it turns you into an addict.

So was he really useless? A tag-along? An extra wheel that never touched the ground? Yes. For the people outside, and the others not under cartel hold, he didn't have much of anything to offer. But that wasn't a bad thing. Baker had reframed the situation, and knew he shouldn't feel shitty about himself because of it. He had never planned to be an asset. His ultimate goal was to screw over everyone and get back to his wife.

Refocused, Baker finished his taco and brushed off the half of it that had dribbled down the front of his shirt. The only person he cared about being a team with was waiting for him back in The States. It was time to get that back into the forefront of his thoughts and start his moves to complete his original plan.

While Ernie was wrong about him being more of a spectator than a participant, he was right that Baker needed to change that perception. Not truly help the team, but help enough to get them to the point where he could backstab them and run off with whatever was hidden on the ocean floor.

And there was only one way he could think of to do that.

He heard the conversation as he got to the first floor. Ernie was arguing with Diego about trusting a kid over himself. Rick was silent, as he had been since they'd gone outside. Rick wasn't a chatterbox, but Baker knew something was up. Something Rick was holding back. And it didn't take a field agent to figure out what it might be. Sitting at a desk and analyzing data all day, people's movements and actions, gave Baker that extra edge.

"...Because you're putting your trust into a kid instead of grown adults who know what they're doing," Ernie said as Baker came outside.

"He's not just some child from the streets. He's my child. Our child," Diego said, pointing between him and Maria.

"All the more reason not to trust anything he says. Look at his parents."

"You better watch your mouth, Ernesto. I wouldn't be talking about the trustworthiness of someone's kids when your daughter is out doing who knows what to try to sabotage me."

"Look, there's no reason to argue right now. Maybe the Nacho knows something, maybe he's just saying that because he's being dressed down by a couple known cartel members. The fact is, we can help you with this, just as planned." Rick sat forward in his chair. "JoJo is out there with Cuba basically diving every little section of ocean around here. You don't have to keep us here. Let me go and get back to them. The second they find something, I can alert you. It's better than having your men tail Cuba. He'd sniff that out in a second."

"There is another option," Baker said. Everyone turned to him, looking at him as if they just realized he was around.

"And what's that, DEA man?" Diego asked.

"You can keep letting your son play in the pool, eat his treats, and act like the child he is. You don't have to get him involved at all. It doesn't matter if he knows where the treasure is anymore."

"It doesn't? And why not?"

"Because Rick here knows. Your kid has been hanging on his coattails like Oliver Twist looking for a parent. Nacho told Rick sure as the sun is a blazing inferno around here. You want to know? Let me drag it out of him."

"If what you say is true, my men could do that."

"Oh sure, they can torture him until he gives up some info. Whether it's true or not, who would know? Torture tends to be a impetus for story telling. Let me deal with him. The way I know. The way I was taught. I'll get that location for you. All I want is a fair cut and safe passage out of this country."

TWENTY-THREE

If there was any more treasure in the sand, it was buried deep enough no one would be able to find it without the proper equipment. Catalina supposed she could purchase metal detectors in the future and find out if there was more to be claimed.

Maybe she could tell Ignacio she'd left some back at the beach so he'd think she hadn't stolen all of it.

Arturo was sleeping soundly on the floor at her feet and she knew she could easily kill him. Slit his throat and leave him here with the other dead boys.

But she needed Arturo to move the rest of the treasure and it was right about time for them to make another run at it.

"Wake up. Grab a wheelbarrow and the tools," Catalina said, kicking Arturo lightly in the side until he opened his eyes. "Time to get the rest of the treasure. Hurry."

Within minutes they had two wheelbarrows and all the tools covered with tarps inside, and headed back to the beach. It was dark and the moon was hidden in the clouds above, which worked perfectly to cover their passage.

A couple of times a vehicle came down the road and they ducked into an alley and waited for it to pass. There was no one on the street but that didn't mean there weren't eyes watching them.

They exchanged no words. That had been the plan. Voices carried.

Catalina thought she heard someone approaching from behind at one point, but when she turned she saw no one. She hoped she was just being paranoid and they weren't being followed.

The beach was empty and they immediately went into the surf with their tools. The tide was higher than it had been when they'd first started taking the treasure, but Catalina knew they'd be able to crack open the remaining chests and pull out the loot.

Gold and jewelry doesn't float away, she thought with a smile.

"What's so funny?" Arturo whispered.

Catalina shook her head and got to work.

The next chest cracked open, a seam splintering down the middle of the top and exposing many gold-encrusted items.

"Wow," Arturo said, yanking a large golden cross from the chest. "It's so heavy. Worth millions, right?"

"Put it in the wheelbarrow," Catalina said and shook her head. "We need to hurry."

Arturo did as he was told and they began pulling everything from the first chest, Catalina holding the flashlight with one hand and pushing Arturo to work faster.

They filled both wheelbarrows within an hour but there were at least two more chests deeper in the surf.

"We'll have to come back for these at low tide tomorrow," Catalina said. "Time to get back to the warehouse."

They packed up their tools and covered everything with the tarps.

Arturo was in the lead as they managed to get moving in the right direction, and once they got off of the sand it was much easier to push and steer.

They were halfway back when Catalina was sure there was someone following them now. She turned quickly and saw a small dark figure duck behind a building down the street.

"We have company," Catalina said to Arturo. "Keep going. I'm going to see who it is."

Catalina turned her wheelbarrow into the nearest alley and waited. She made sure the Glock was still loaded.

A minute later she heard someone coming down the road and peeked out.

It was two of the street urchins, Tomas and Jose.

Catalina stepped out, scaring both boys. "What are you following me for?"

"No, we're not. We're, uh... working. Like Arturo told us to do. Seeing if anyone is around, you know?" Jose looked down at his feet as he spoke. Obviously lying.

"Go home. Arturo is with me and we don't need any help," Catalina said.

Neither boy moved or said a word.

"Did he tell you to follow us?" Catalina asked.

"No, no. I mean, we've been out here all night because that's what we are supposed to be doing," Jose said.

Tomas smiled. "Do you need our help? Whatever you're pushing seems to be heavy. We could help. We want to do our part."

Catalina wished they'd stepped out on the way to the beach because then she could have had two more wheelbarrows in play and maybe gotten the rest of the treasure.

"No. Go away. Arturo will find you tomorrow and give you more work." Catalina waved her hands and the two boys slowly walked down the street. Once they were far enough away, she got back to pushing the treasure.

Catalina got back to the warehouse, where Arturo was already sorting the items they'd found. He helped her move the rest of it to the section they were working in.

"Did you have Tomas and Jose follow me?" Catalina asked.

Arturo frowned. "No. Why? Did you run into them?"

"Yes. They told me you told them to do it." Catalina knew that wasn't exactly what had been said but she was mad they'd been following. She wondered if they'd seen them go to the beach and see what they were doing.

Maybe they're heading to the beach right now, she thought.

"I'll be right back," Catalina said. She had the Glock in her hand. "I need to be able to trust you, but I don't. Not yet. Come with me and hurry."

"Where are we going?"

Catalina motioned with the Glock for Arturo to follow, and she ran out of the warehouse and down the street.

If she found Tomas and Jose on the beach she would have no choice but to kill them, and then kill Arturo. No one was going to get the rest of the treasure but her. In the end, she'd be the one who had it all to herself.

They got to the beach but it was empty. Catalina was relieved but also annoyed.

She realized she was hoping the two boys would be in the surf, dragging the rest of the treasure to shore. Catalina would let them do it and then force them to bring it back to the warehouse.

Then she would kill Tomas and Jose before killing Arturo.

"See. We're wasting time," Arturo said.

Catalina felt the anger rise inside and turned toward Arturo. "You don't talk to me like that."

"Like what?"

Catalina shot Arturo twice in the chest and watched him fall.

"Like that," she said, and sighed. Now she'd have to do the rest of the work on her own.

She grabbed Arturo's leg and began dragging him down the beach, hoping to find a spot to bury his body so no one would find it or the treasure.

TWENTY-FOUR

"Captain Jonah, at your service, sir." The man was as big as a house, with rippling muscles underneath his camouflage uniform. His arms were gigantic, and they were swelling from holding the gigantic machine gun.

"Excellent. The others should be here soon enough," Cuba said. "Why don't you go and pick your quarters, captain? We have much to do but first we'll talk."

The man shook his head. "Not much for talking. I let the music do the talking, if you know what I mean."

Cuba frowned. "There are sixteen other soldiers that should be arriving in the next three days or so. Once everyone is assembled we'll get a game plan and then you can do what you do best."

"Negative. I am here to do what needs to be done. Not worry about others, sir. You give me a target and before the others arrive I'll have this area cleared of your enemies." Captain Jonah grinned. "I just need a cigar and you to point me in the right direction."

"I hired a team of men to do this work," Cuba said. He was still feeling the effects of all the alcohol he'd been drinking, nonstop, the last day or three. "There are a few enemies I need eliminated."

"Excellent. Give me the list and in the order you'd like them to be eliminated," Captain Jonah said. "Of course, depending on the circumstances, there might be one or two flipped in the wrong order. I'll do my best to take them out however you'd like them gone."

"You're the damn Grim Reaper," Cuba said.

"I am Death. I should get my own book. Maybe someday they'll write about my exploits, but I doubt it. I do much better work when no one knows I exist." Captain Jonah hefted the machine gun over his shoulder. "I'll need my list. I want to be finished in the next twenty-four hours if possible. My daughter has her first recital and I promised her I would be there."

Cuba was dumbfounded. "You have a child?"

Captain Jonah nodded. "I do. If you'll hold my weapon I can show you a picture of her."

"No, I believe you." Cuba didn't think he could hold onto the massive machine gun long enough to see what this man was a father to.

"Then I just need the list," Captain Jonah said.

"How will you move around Mexico without drawing so much attention, and how did you get that weapon into the country?" Cuba asked.

"I have my ways." Captain Jonah frowned. "I need the list. You don't want me to become impatient. This is never about the money. This is about the hunt. It's not the kill, it's the thrill of the chase."

Cuba shrugged. "Is that some poetic lines you learned?"

"Deep Purple. The rock band. It's from their lyrics," Captain Jonah said.

Cuba felt a massive headache coming on. "Do I just tell you the names or write them down or what?"

"I'd prefer a written list with as much information about each as possible, if that works for you."

Cuba shrugged again. "I guess it will have to, right? I need to find a pen and paper. Would you like a drink? I have some rum and some bourbon left."

"Do you have an energy drink? I could use a Red Bull."

"No, I don't use mixers. I prefer to drink straight from the bottle," Cuba said.

"Why?"

Cuba thought about the question. "I guess I'm becoming an alcoholic."

"You should be careful. It seems like you already have enough problems since you're paying me to kill multiple people," Captain Jonah said. "Just saying."

A pen and a sheet of paper was found in a drawer. Cuba didn't know where everything was yet. He'd only rented this new villa within the hour, expecting this goon and the others to arrive either late tonight or early morning.

Cuba wrote down everyone's name he knew, but then added *any Sinaloa Cartel member* at the bottom of the list. Better to be safe than sorry.

He handed it to Captain Jonah, who stared at the list. "Is this the right order?"

"Yes, it doesn't really matter. Most of them will be together anyway." Cuba sat down on the nearest chair. "Oh, wait... no, no..." He groaned. "I need one of them alive."

"Which one?"

Cuba thought about it. "Grace. She needs to be brought back to me."

"I can do that." Captain Jonah tore the sheet of paper up and stuffed the pieces into his mouth.

"What are you doing?"

"Destroying the evidence, and it helps me to absorb the information better. Kill everyone but Grace, and as many cartel members as I can find. How far do you need me to go?" Captain Jonah switched the machine gun to his other shoulder.

"If cartel members get between you and the main list, then take them out. I don't need you to travel from Mexico to Colombia and take out every cartel member," Cuba said.

"Not this trip. I have the recital, but feel free to hire me when you need that done. I charge per person, as you know, and I'll add every cartel member at half price. They're never too tough. Lots of talk, lots of waving guns and yelling Spanish, but in the end they fall when you put a bullet between their beady eyes." Captain Jonah grinned again.

"The one on the list, Diego, is the one I need dead. He's a bigwig in the cartel, and so is Maria. Those two dead should mess them up a bit," Cuba said. "The rest are because I don't like them."

"If you want me to be subtle about this, make it look like a series of accidents, that will cost you extra." Captain Jonah put the machine gun down on the floor, leaning against his thick leg.

Cuba shook his head.

"It doesn't matter how they die. I just want them dead. Got it? They blew up my villa." Cuba fought to keep his eyes open. He needed a twelve-hour power nap soon.

Captain Jonah looked around. "They didn't do too bad of a job, unless they were the ones to add those ridiculous statues out front."

"Not this villa. The last one," Cuba said. "Anyway, go and kill them all. I need to sleep."

"Sure, not a problem." Captain Jonah picked up his machine gun and threw it over his shoulder and started to turn before putting a finger up. "Oh, maybe one problem."

"What is it?"

"I have no clue where to look for them, what they look like or who is helping them. I think I would know what Grace looked like but maybe not. There might be hundreds of tourists in Mexico that look like a Grace. I'd hate to have to kill them all, or worse... accidentally kill your Grace, when you want her alive."

Cuba sighed. "Give me a second. I need another drink."

"I think you might have a problem," Captain Jonah said.

Cuba had to agree with the man. He had many, many problems.

TWENTY-FIVE

Alberto was trying to stay away from Cuba as much as possible. JoJo appeared to have just taken it upon herself to disappear whenever she wanted. He figured since Cuba could no longer trust her, she decided she couldn't get into any more issues with him.

She was wrong. Cuba was losing control, big time, and a man like that is dangerous when everything falls apart.

The only way for Cuba to regain control was to take out everyone who was a part of the mess and begin again. Alberto wasn't sure if he was a part of the problem. He hoped that his display the other morning when he swore his loyalty to Cuba was enough to keep a gun off his back.

Just in case, Alberto was spending a lot of time down at the beach, tinkering with his boat. Pretending to be busy while inwardly freaking out, trying to come to a decision as to what he should do.

He'd bought a bucket of beer from the beach bar and was close to finishing it up when he noticed a man strolling down his way. Alberto reached for his gun and tucked it under his shirt. The man could be some tourist taking a stroll, but after these past events Alberto couldn't be too cautious.

He pretended to be adjusting the equipment at the back of the boat, but was keeping an eye on the man as he got closer. He wasn't sure if his vision was bouncing because of the incoming swells or the six beers in his gut.

The man walked by, gave him a short nod which Alberto returned, and kept going down the beach.

I really need to start calming down, Alberto thought.

But he knew it would take a while for his brain to start processing the world normally again. If he made it out of this alive. Right now that was all he was concerned about. Afterwards, when the smoke settled, he would focus on rebuilding the life he'd made for himself in this town.

Alberto had to cancel all upcoming boat tours and fishing expeditions when Cuba had taken it upon himself to requisition him and his boat. He could only imagine the negative reviews on Yelp and other sites he was getting. His business wasn't just taking a hit financially. He could recover from that. But online reviews and word of mouth were killers.

It had been over a day since he'd seen Cuba. Yesterday was the first time since he'd been roped into this treasure hunt that Cuba hadn't forced everyone out on the water to dive.

He was glad for the day off, but the sudden break in schedule worried him. Had Cuba found someone else? If so, would he just let him go, resume life again, or would Alberto turn the key on the boat one day and go up in a fireball?

Maybe it was time to bite the bullet and drive off into the horizon. Take the boat to Cuba, or the Dominican and reinvent himself. He'd done it before, so would have no issues doing it again.

If Cuba no longer needed him, then he would rather disappear on his own than have someone else make him disappear.

Alberto grabbed the bucket of empty beers and stepped off the boat. Today he would get drunk, and tomorrow morning would decide what path to take.

And if Cuba showed up, so what? It would just be more of the same.

The bar had gotten busy since he first dropped in, busier than he'd seen it in a while. It took him a moment to realize how much time had passed. Tourist season was kicking in. That solo man walking the beach would soon turn into a few dozen people kicking up sand and tossing their garbage everywhere.

He made his way through the crowd, apologizing to the people he bumped into even though it wasn't his fault. He didn't need to have a day away from Cuba only to get pummeled by a handful of frat boy assholes.

Alberto went to the side of the bar where the clean-up station was and propped his bucket on the counter. The bartender was running around like crazy trying to keep up with the crowd. They were earlier in the season than normal. The owner probably thought he had time before needing to hire a second person.

That wouldn't be a bad idea, Alberto thought.

He could go someplace really tropical. Get a tiki hut on the beach and serve beautiful women in scant bikinis and serve fruity drinks with umbrellas in them. Alberto barely knew how to pour a beer, let alone some island beverage, but not knowing never stopped him before. He'd learn on the job, just like everything else he had done.

"Hi sailor," a voice said next to him.

Alberto turned and jumped a little.

"Grace. How did you get here? Did the cartel let you go?"

"I excused myself from their presence. Where's my stupid real father at?"

"I'm assuming somewhere getting drunk and plotting a whole lot of violence."

"Things not looking up on the diving for treasure thing, huh?"

"Still coming up empty as usual."

"Well, you're in luck, because I haven't forgotten about us and our plan."

"You said you never had a plan."

Grace shrugged. "There's always a plan, you just have to figure out what it is. Right now, it seems pretty clear to me. We have Daddy Cuba spiraling into chaos because he can't get what he wants. Last I heard, when I was with Diego, is that his plan, eventually, is to go after him. Cuba probably already knows this and is preparing for his own little war. Ernie's playing his usual game of deceit. Rick is going to do whatever JoJo does, and JoJo is on my team right now. Baker, who the hell knows what's up with him. And the kid? Well, he's the one person I wouldn't count out at the moment."

"Why don't you just get out of here? Get on a plane and go home? Once I recover from my hangover tomorrow, I'm probably setting sail myself."

"Why run when we're so close?"

Alberto laughed. "Did you not understand what I said? Nobody knows where this damn treasure is, and a lot of people are going to get killed over something that probably doesn't exist."

"What if I told you it did exist, and I can prove it to you?"

"Then I'd say you better watch your back, because if anyone else finds out you're dead."

Grace reached into her pocket and pulled out something that glinted in the sunlight. She slapped it down on the counter, cupping her hand around it to hide it from the other people in the bar.

"Is that–"

"It is. Found it on the beach not too far from where we'd been staying this whole time. I'm pretty sure Nacho's crew found what we've been looking for and have hidden it somewhere. Kids did what a bunch of adults couldn't do."

"What do we do now, then?"

"The last thing I want to do is confront those street rats. They're more dangerous than they look. We need Nacho away from the cartel and back with us. It's like that bible saying: 'and the little child shall lead them.'"

TWENTY-SIX

"Time to leave, Nacho." It was Rick standing over Ignacio and he looked scared. "Hurry up."

Ignacio rolled out of bed and slipped his shoes on quickly. "Where are we going?"

"Away from here. There's talk on the street. Your crew double-crossed you. Wandering around town in the middle of the night with wheelbarrows, coming and going from the beach area. Sounds like something to be worried about?"

Ignacio groaned. "Catalina. I told her."

Rick shook his head. "You can never trust a woman. Am I right? Anyway, we need to find her and see if she stole the treasure out from under us, which is the most likely scenario. Things are moving at a fast clip, Nacho, so we need to get ahead of it. Before it's too late."

Ignacio was embarrassed. He'd let his feelings for Catalina get in the way. Now they might have lost the treasure, and there was no one else to blame but himself.

"I'm so sorry, Rick."

Rick frowned. "Hey, shit happens, Nacho. This is what life's all about. You think I wanted this for my life, this late in life? Hell no. I should be retiring from a solid FBI career and playing with my grandkids. Not having to wake a kid out of bed somewhere in the armpit of Mexico because there's missing treasure."

Ignacio knew Rick was trying to make him feel better. He'd need to push aside his self-loathing and figure out how to get the treasure from Catalina, and see who else was involved. He knew beyond a shadow of a doubt that Arturo was also going to have his hand in this.

"How are we going to get out?" Ignacio asked.

"We're going to slip out through the kitchen door and across the backyard, past the pool area and over the fence," Rick said. He smiled. "Pretty simple, really."

"I wish we could walk out the front door like everyone else seems to do," Ignacio said. He turned to his bed and fluffed his pillows up as well as molding his blankets so it looked like he was still in bed. If someone walked into his room they'd see the ruse immediately, but to a casual glance it might just work.

Rick took Ignacio by the hand and led him out into the hallway, stopping to listen for anyone moving. When it was obvious they were alone, for the moment, the pair began to move quickly but quietly down the hall to the far end and the stairwell.

Satisfied there wasn't a guard lingering in the stairwell, they began their descent to the first floor.

At the bottom, Rick put his hand on the door but instead of opening he turned to Ignacio. "If we're seen I'll give myself up. That means you need to get out of the villa and over the wall. Find Catalina and figure out where she's hiding the treasure. Then come back for me. If I'm not dead I can help you get it all back. Got it?"

Ignacio nodded, but he hoped Rick wasn't caught and didn't have to sacrifice himself. He wanted to go with Rick to confront Catalina, because she might have the full might of his crew now.

My former crew, he thought.

Now on the first floor, Rick opened the door and began moving toward the kitchen area. "If anyone asks, we're going for a late-night snack."

Ignacio didn't know if Rick was joking or not. If anyone saw the two of them sneaking around they'd know this was an escape attempt.

They walked into the kitchen and Ignacio bumped into Rick, who'd stopped suddenly.

Diego was seated at the table with a plate of melon he was slicing with a very large knife.

Ignacio saw the Glock near his elbow on the table, too.

"Ahh, guests. Did you smell the delicious melon I'm preparing?" Diego asked.

Rick cleared his throat but didn't say anything.

Diego pointed with the knife at the other end of the table. "Sit. Join me. I insist."

Rick sat across from Diego, who pointed at Ignacio with the knife. "Before you sit, little one, come and get some of this melon for you and your friend."

Ignacio did as he was told. Diego simply handed him a couple of pieces of melon.

Diego took a bite of melon and put the knife down. "So... which one of you wants to tell me where you were headed this time of night? The streets of Mexico, and especially this town, are very dangerous. About to get even more dangerous."

Ignacio glanced at Rick, who returned the look.

"We were heading here, to the kitchen, to get–"

Diego swept up the Glock and shook his head. "You get one lie. That was it. I have no problem shooting you, Rick. You mean nothing to me."

"What about me?" Ignacio asked.

Diego smiled and put the weapon back down. "I need you to tell me the truth."

"I think the treasure has been found and stolen," Ignacio said.

Rick groaned quietly next to him, but there was nothing else to do but tell the truth. More than likely, Diego already had word about it if Rick knew.

"And you know who has done this?" Diego asked.

Ignacio nodded.

"Your street urchins that you lead?"

Ignacio nodded again.

"Fine. Then finish your melon. We will go together, all of us. Even Rick. He might come in handy. I'll assemble several of my men for backup." Diego took another bite.

Rick waved his hands. "We don't need armed backup. They're a bunch of dirty kids. We can get the treasure without using force."

"No, I'm not worried about the children. They are the least of our problems," Diego said. "You forget who I am. What information I get in real time. You see, while you two were upstairs plotting to get the treasure and run off together, I was gathering intel about a large group of armed men landing in town and heading in our direction. Your friend, Cuba, has hired several American killers to take us all out. All of us."

"What are you going to do about it?" Rick asked.

Diego shrugged. "I have a dozen of my own armed killers, and another three dozen heading in this direction. I have so many cartel members within driving distance. This new threat will be dealt with quickly and severely. All you need to worry about is getting me the treasure."

"And then what about us?" Ignacio asked.

Diego smiled and took another bite. "And then I give everyone a small token payment and you get out of my Mexico and never return."

TWENTY-SEVEN

Maria never slept well, even when she was at one of her own places and not in a strange house surrounded by men who had no interest in protecting her.

As quiet as he tried to be, she heard Rick open his bedroom door, whisper to someone, and start down the stairs. Not the best start to an obvious escape attempt. Though, if that dopey white girl got off the property without being seen, they could probably escape while shooting revolvers into the air and singing folk songs.

Maria got dressed and followed them downstairs. She listened around the corner from the kitchen as Diego stopped them and they discussed the situation.

She should have guessed that Diego would be up and waiting for someone to try to leave. She may not like him, despite how they used to feel about each other in the past, but he was always one step ahead of everyone else. It was the reason he'd gotten to where he was in the cartel. This thought led to another one: maybe he let Grace go.

The girl didn't seem like she was going to be much help for him. He'd probably be better off without her around, so just let her escape. She wouldn't go to the police. A girl like that, growing up with Ernie Patek as a father, would know that calling the cops wasn't even a last choice. Besides, those uniforms had been bought a long time ago. They would have detained her and called Diego to come get her.

Maria let them leave, hiding in the shadows as they left the kitchen. She didn't want to jump in on them and invite herself along, just another body in the group. She had no desire to help them find anything.

This girl that Ignacio trusted with the location of the treasure, she must be taken care of. Two men and a boy? The first thing they were going to focus on was the treasure. That was the wrong move, and that's why women like her would always have the upper hand. Greed had a place close to the top of everyone's life, where it belonged. But there were times when it needed to be pushed down that ladder.

The girl, Catalina, was obviously smart. She'd put on a front strong enough to get Ignacio to do something he normally wouldn't have done. She'd tricked him into revealing the location of the treasure and then backstabbed him the second she had the chance – another thing women were good for.

Catalina needed to go first. Then the treasure. She had disrespected not only the leader of her gang, but a member of Maria's family. Revenge took precedence over greed.

Besides, Maria was pretty sure she knew where the treasure might be. After all, she had run with the town's street gang back in the day. So had Diego. But Diego didn't know about the secret space the girls in the gang used to go to in order to be girls and not just tough brutes all the time.

If Ignacio's gang had kept the same territory and not let anything change, then Maria would bet the treasure was there. And since there was no way Catalina would have dug up and transported it from wherever it was found to the secret spot, it meant that she'd given away the location by bringing boys into it. Another reason she needed to die.

Maria didn't see the difference between killing someone young or old. They were all just people. Sparing the life of a child just because she was a child was not only stupid, but showed weakness.

She went back upstairs and packed some items into a small tote bag. She didn't rush it, but wasn't taking her time either. She didn't want to run into Diego as she was leaving. He probably put a couple of his men on higher alert since he wouldn't be in the building. This meant she would need to be a little more careful. She wouldn't just be able to walk out.

Since Diego and the other two had left through the front door, Maria decided to take the side. Unfortunately, when she entered the kitchen to leave, a guard was already standing in front of the way out.

"You're going to keep me inside on this beautiful night?" Maria asked.

"Nobody goes out. Orders from the boss."

"Do you know who I am?"

The guard hesitated, then nodded before pulling up on his weapon as if it was a safety blanket.

"Then you know what I can have done to you. And you know if I tell you to move, as your superior, you have to fucking move."

"Sorry, Miss Maria. Orders from Mr. Santiago. I answer to him, not you. He will do a lot worse if I let you out."

"Soldier, you have no idea what I can have done to you. But fine. Just wanted to take in the stars, the fresh air. I guess I'm shit out of luck."

Maria turned toward the kitchen island. She looked at the fruit bowl and the plate of half eaten melon slices.

"I guess I'll have a late night snack instead. Do you want some?" She gestured at the fruit. Diego had a habit of only letting his men eat once a day. Something about them being more alert on empty stomachs.

The guard hesitated and shook his head, then looked behind him as if Diego would be staring at him from outside.

"Just you and me here. And unless you rat on yourself, I'm not saying anything so nobody else will find out."

She turned back to the plate as the guard came up behind her. When Maria felt his breath on the back of her head, she grabbed the pocket knife Diego had left on the island and spun. She got the guard a half a dozen times in the stomach before he started to react. By that time, it was too late, and she jammed the blade into his neck, pulling it out and dodging the arterial spray.

Unlike the American movies, it only takes a few seconds for someone to bleed out from that type of neck wound. By the time the person instinctively reaches for their neck, their vision is going out, and they're on the floor dead before they can put together what happened.

Maria checked herself. Other than a little splatter on her sleeve, and a decent amount on her stabbing hand, she was pretty clean.

She washed the blood off her hand and headed outside. She had expected another guard at the door built into the hedges that led to the side parking area, but nobody was there. Diego probably thought guarding the house exits was enough.

Maria walked off the property. She'd been to the house enough in the past, when her and Diego were still a thing, and was able to navigate her way through the woods, staying off the main road but keeping it in sight.

Just before dawn, she made it to town, coming out behind a row of single-story cinder-block homes with clothes still on the line. During her street rat days, part of staying in the crew was being able to know all the twists and turns, alleys and passages throughout the town. The information was burnt into her memory and it only took a minute to navigate the maze of clustered housing before reaching the main road.

She didn't know where this Catalina girl lived, but she was almost certain she knew where she would be heading to when she awoke. And Maria would make sure she'd be waiting there for her.

TWENTY-EIGHT

Catalina had loaded the wheelbarrow twice more, taking the bigger objects the first time and then as much of the scattered coins the second.

It was getting too bright out, the sun shining obnoxiously over the horizon already. No time to do another pass at the treasure, but Catalina was sure she could finish getting the rest of it tonight if she started early enough.

Catalina wondered if she should quit while she was ahead. She knew she'd never be able to move all of it from the warehouse. Her hope was to be able to keep it there without anyone stumbling upon it. She could move a few items at a time and bring home some of the gold and silver coins in her pockets each day. She wondered what her mother would say, and if she'd tell anyone else in the family.

Her uncles and aunts could not be trusted. No, Catalina decided to keep this hidden from her mother as long as possible. She'd need to find someone outside of town to move the treasure without screwing her over, or at least someone who'd be able to melt the gold down so she could sell it by weight.

While some of the items were really nice to look at, she didn't think she'd need a gold, silver and jeweled crown to wear. Better to break it apart and sell it off and get the most money for it.

Catalina needed to dispose of the bodies, too. The smell might attract someone to investigate, and she could already see some rats hanging around, too. The cockroaches and other creatures would fill the warehouse shortly unless she did something about the dead boys.

Arturo had been dragged up the beach and buried under a dead tree, but he'd be found sooner than later. The hope was Catalina had buried him so far away from the treasure chests no one would put two and two together and find both.

What can I do now except go home and sleep? I need to get some food in me and figure out what I need to do, Catalina thought.

Having millions of dollars in front of her meant nothing right now. She was a kid, and any adult who got wind of this would try to take it from her. She worried her own family would be so greedy they'd take it all and do something stupid with it, like show it off. Flaunt it around town.

Get every last one of them killed.

Catalina knew there would be many questions. The cartel would come looking for her, if they weren't already on her trail. Ignacio might already have told them what had happened, if he'd gone to the chests in the last day or two and saw what had happened to some of the treasure.

She filled her pockets with some of the coins and left the warehouse, making sure to lock up behind her.

On the streets, the town was emerging from sleep, people heading to work or to start their day.

Catalina nodded at a few people she knew, gave a quick wave here and there, and tried to act as normal as she could. No use in anyone seeing her being any different than normal days.

When she got home, her mother was still asleep in her bedroom.

Catalina found some leftover meat and cheese from last night's dinner she'd missed, and took out a couple of tortillas. She'd scramble some eggs with the meat and cheese and have a good breakfast.

Her mother woke to the smell of the food cooking, coming out and making herself a cup of tea. "Where were you all night? Running with that horrible gang of yours?"

"No, mama. I was... I was doing something good for us."

Her mother frowned. "Like what? Make me some food, too."

"Yes, ma'am."

As Catalina added more food to the skillet, she knew her mother was staring at her. Waiting for an answer to where she'd been and what she'd done. Unlike most of the other members of the crew, Catalina had it good. Her mother cared about her. While she'd never be called a great mother, she at least asked questions. Catalina had no curfew, but she was questioned when she stayed out all night.

Her mother also had a bad drinking problem, like nearly everyone in the family. Catalina could smell the tequila even from this distance, her mother sweating out the toxins.

"Tell me what you've done," her mother said.

"Nothing. I–"

"There's blood on your pant leg and your shoe," her mother said quietly.

It was so quiet, Catalina turned to look at her mother's bloodshot eyes. They were welling with tears.

"What have you done, child?"

Catalina turned her head and went back to cooking. "It's from a cat I accidentally hit with a bike. Nothing important."

"Lies."

Catalina's hands were shaking. Her mother was anything but stupid, even with a hangover. She'd get the information from her daughter.

"I think I found a way for us to get out of this town. Out of Mexico. Buy our way to a new life in the United States," Catalina said.

"How?" Her mother stood, the chair scraping across the wooden floor. "Tell me how you can do this. I want the truth, young lady, or else."

Catalina knew her mother was bluffing, because she'd never do anything like a spanking or punishment. But that wasn't really the point.

"Let me show you," Catalina said, and waved for her mother to sit. The food was done and she began plating it. "Can you make me a cup of coffee, please and thank you, ma'am?"

They hovered around one another in the small kitchen for a couple of minutes, getting the table set, the drinks poured and then saying Grace before they ate.

"Now tell me," her mother said, taking a bite of her food. She smacked her lips and Catalina knew she'd done well with the food.

Catalina took a bite. She didn't realize how hungry she was, but she'd not slept more than a few minutes here and there and had burned a lot of energy moving the treasure.

"Here. I have these," Catalina said and took a handful of the gold coins from her pocket and put them on the table between her and her mother.

"What..." Her mother picked up a coin and held it up in front of her face. "Is it real?"

"Yes, ma'am. They are all real. Worth a lot of money. Worth our freedom," Catalina said. "Please don't ask me where I got them."

Her mother counted the coins. "Are there more?"

Catalina emptied her pockets and watched as her mother counted the coins. "There are more, too. A lot more."

Her mother stared at Catalina. "How many more? Twice this amount?"

Catalina smiled. "Half a dozen wheelbarrows full. Not only coins but golden items like crowd and jewelry and–"

"I'm going to get your uncles and you're going to show us," her mother said.

Catalina shook her head. "No. This is mine. I'm not sharing it with them. They'll take it because they are greedy. They'll tell the cartel and then we'll all be dead."

Her mother stood and scooped up the coins, putting them in her pocket. "You will tell me right now where–"

The knock at the door shut them both up.

TWENTY-NINE

JoJo knew how to tell when things were about to crash down, blow up, when plans collapsed and took someone's sanity with it. She'd been in on multiple failed cons, grifts, and heists that, while they may not have gone south, took close friends with it down in flames.

JoJo knew how to spot the tells.

However, Cuba made it easy for her. He obviously wasn't trying to hide what he probably considered his failsafe: drop the hunt, take out everyone involved, and re-group with new people and a better semblance of a plan. With the amount of armed men coming in and out of the new house, you could be dead and still figure out what was going on.

She'd snuck up close to the place to see if Alberto was still there. He'd claimed he was just playing Cuba, but someone who said that could easily be duping both sides.

Alberto never came off as very dangerous, so JoJo wasn't too worried about him on his own. But if he was really on Cuba's side and all he told her was just talk, that made Cuba even more of a threat.

Not that he wasn't already. These armed men were different from the ones he had used previously who acted more as guards than anything. The way these men moved was more like trained soldiers. People trained not only in warfare but in ignoring any moral code of ethics most military people had.

Mercenaries. Murderers. Maniacs.

This could only mean one thing: everyone who had come into contact with Cuba during his gold-fever treasure hunting frenzy were about to find themselves looking at the business end of a gun.

Alberto could already be inside the house, long dead. JoJo, when it came down to it, really just cared about herself and Rick. She liked Alberto. Hell, she even liked Grace, as much as she didn't want to admit it. But when a small army is gearing up to start a small war in a previously quiet Mexican beach town, the only people that mattered were the ones you cared about the most.

Rick was in the cartel's hands for the moment, which was a plus for him. JoJo never thought she would think that, but she figured if Cuba was going to take on Diego and his men, he wouldn't make it first priority. He'd make sure Grace, Alberto, Baker, and the rest were gone and then storm wherever Diego was.

JoJo needed to get word to Rick somehow to get out of there and as far away from town as possible. She would meet him wherever he went and then they'd get the hell out of Dodge. Neither of them could go back to The States, since they both were still listed as Most Wanted and probably will be for the rest of their lives. But they could head further south, deeper into the lands of non-extradition.

She had no idea how she could get a message to Rick, though. No idea where he was, or who had any connections to find out. There was the Maria chick, but JoJo didn't know where she was. She also didn't trust her.

Alberto might know, but again he might be a corpse sitting a few hundred feet in front of her. And if he wasn't and had left Cuba, he should be smart enough to be long gone on his boat.

The kid maybe? But where the hell would she find him? In the past, Nacho always found her wherever she was just to annoy her. But she had the feeling, the way everyone in their strange circle had been doing lately, that it wouldn't be as easy this time.

JoJo was about to break down in tears from the hopelessness she felt in this situation. This was the first time in a long time that she'd felt completely on her own. Which made her think of Grace. Which made her remember that Grace could get in contact with Ernie with those creepy earrings he'd given her. If JoJo could get to Grace, she would be able to pass the word, through Ernie, to Rick and maybe they all would have a chance to get out of here alive.

Now she just needed to find out where Grace was. They'd separated after finding the coin on the beach and had plans to meet up later in the day to put together a plan. But JoJo didn't want to wait until then. The treasure wasn't as valuable as her life at this point. The sooner she got to Grace and in contact with Ernie, the sooner she could have Rick at her side and disappear.

JoJo backed up deeper into the copse she was partially hidden in. She cursed as a branch from a tree poked into her back.

"Do we have a Peeping Tom here?" a voice said from behind her.

The gun she had mistaken as a branch creeped lower on her back to just above her waistline. JoJo froze and sucked in a deep breath.

"Turn around," the voice said.

She turned slowly, putting her hands in front of her in case the guy behind her thought she was reaching for something. She figured one of Cuba's new militia men had snuck around and caught her from behind, but the man she faced was, if part of Cuba's new team, the jacked up Hulk of all of them.

Despite the heat, no sweat dotted his face or arms. He appeared completely in control of himself, even to the point of ignoring the weather. His arms looked like thick ropes twisting around each other. He was cut without having to flex. Worst of all, his face was one of sereneness, not the type that put you at ease but the kind that confirmed you were looking at an individual with no conscience at all.

His eyes scared her more than Cuba or the cartel.

"Well, you must be JoJo. I can see what Cuba saw in you. It'll be a shame to ruin that face of yours. But maybe we'll have some fun before I put a bullet between your eyes."

"You must be the guy who's supposed to take out all of us."

"Nothing gets past you, does it? Let's go." The man gestured toward the house.

"Why are we going there? Wouldn't it be easier for you to just kill me and let me rot right here?"

A strange sense of calm had come over JoJo. Something in her accepted that this was the last act of her life and calmed the panic that had welled up. She felt similar whenever she got on an airplane. She had never been a good flier, anxious up until the moment the plane's wheels left the ground. Then, her body relaxed, knowing that at the moment she no longer had control over what was going to happen next. It was giving into fate.

"Usually I would, but being so close to the house and all, I think it might score me brownie points to bring you in. Cuba definitely has a thing for you. He almost told me not to come after you, just take out the rest of your friends. But he's a rare kind of man who doesn't let his dick get in the way of what's important."

"Well, let's go then. I assume you want me to lead the way? You can take point if you want."

"Very funny. You wouldn't be able to jump me from behind anyway. Now move."

JoJo crossed the road to the driveway, her mind spinning. Since she wasn't dead yet, that meant she might still find a way out of this new predicament. She just needed enough time to find out what that was.

THIRTY

"Arturo is missing, and so are some of the others."

Catalina nodded, blocking the doorway to her apartment. She didn't want any of the street urchins to enter, worried her mother would show them the coins and think everyone in town was going to be rich.

Only I'm going to be rich, Catalina thought. Already she'd decided to get the coins back from her mother and skip town as soon as possible, once she could liquidate the treasure and find safe passage out of Mexico.

Her mother was going to be trouble and now Catalina wished she'd never showed her the coins.

Just like Ignacio should have never showed me the chests, she thought.

"They're missing," the boy said again, waving his hand in front of Catalina's face. "What are we going to do?"

"We'll need to find them," she said and frowned. "Go find them."

"We've been looking for a couple of hours. Arturo was supposed to give us assignments this morning and he never showed up."

Now it was Catalina's turn to frown. "Why didn't you ask Ignacio? He's in charge again."

The boy sighed. "And where is Ignacio, then? He's also missing. A few of us have bad feelings about things. Feeling some kinda way. You know?"

Catalina did know, but it wasn't the same angle as they were thinking. She knew if she wasn't careful, this would all get so out of control she'd never be able to get out of town with the treasure. "Then look again. They can't have gone too far."

"There are a lot of armed men in town now," one of the others said. "Like, over a dozen of them. Not cartel, either. They're looking for people."

"Like who?" Catalina asked, but she already knew who it was: the group that Ignacio had been working with.

"That gringo Ignacio was always helping out, for starters. They said there's a reward if anyone tells them where he is. They said they only want to talk to him and nothing bad will happen to that man or whoever told him where he is."

Catalina knew that was a lie. If armed men were here they'd be facing off against the cartel as well as killing everyone they were looking for.

She knew Ignacio was going to be caught in the crossfire and she felt bad, but only for a second.

I need to do what needs to be done and quickly, Catalina thought. "Meet me somewhere in two hours. I think I know where everyone is, and Arturo and I have begun something already. Two hours." She flashed them two fingers and went back inside, locking the door.

"Mama, where are you?" Catalina went into her mother's bedroom and saw the woman putting the coins into one of her socks in a drawer. "I want those back."

"You said you had more. Much more," her mother said. "I'm going to invite your uncles over for dinner and we'll figure this all out." She smiled at Catalina. "You did the right thing bringing these to me."

"No, I did the wrong thing. You're going to get us both killed if you tell anyone else, especially from our family," Catalina said. "The Sinaloa Cartel is looking for this treasure. They'll kill all of us and not think about it."

"Then we come up with our own plan," her mother said and shook her head. "I'm not afraid of the cartel and neither are your uncles. In fact, they have many friends in the cartel they can talk to. Make sure nothing bad happens to any of us."

Catalina shook her head. "That won't work. We'll be killed. I cannot stress that part of this enough. Don't you get it? And I don't trust my uncles, either. They'll steal this all from us and disappear, and we'll have to answer for it."

Her mother looked like she'd been slapped. "No, honey, not my brothers. They'll do the right thing. They always do."

"Always?"

Her mother shrugged her shoulders and smiled. "In this case they will. I'll make sure of it."

Catalina was furious, at herself and now at her mother. This was all falling apart.

"I want the coins back," Catalina said.

"You gave them to me. They are now mine. A small part of my fair share." Her mother tried to get past her daughter but Catalina grabbed her mother by the arm.

"They're mine and mine alone." Catalina was gripping her mother's arm as tightly as she could.

"Where did you learn to be so greedy?" Her mother tried to push Catalina's hand off of her arm but couldn't.

"From you. I got this way because of you, you greedy bitch," Catalina said and threw her mother against the bedroom wall, putting her free forearm against her mother's neck and pressing hard. "You're going to get us killed, and I can't have that. You did this to yourself."

As her mother struggled, Catalina got even madder. She kept the pressure on and wouldn't release her grip, even as her mother clawed and scraped her arms, trying to get to her daughter's face and eyes.

"You are the greedy one," Catalina said over and over. As her mother began to slip down the wall, Catalina used it to her advantage and applied even more pressure now that she was standing over her mother.

When her mother stopped fighting and her arms dropped, Catalina counted to twenty and then released her.

Her mother fell to the floor, where Catalina kicked her a few times to make sure the greedy bitch was dead.

She collected the coins from the drawer and left the apartment, vowing never to return. She hoped it would be a few hours before the woman was discovered.

Catalina was going to meet with the rest of the crew at the warehouse. She needed to clean it up so there were no bodies or blood on the ground.

Have them all follow her with wheelbarrows to the beach, where they'd help her collect the rest of the treasure.

Bring it back to the warehouse.

Then Catalina would open fire, killing every last one of them.

She needed their help to do this last thing, but after the treasure was secured she'd need no one. Ever.

Catalina was going to be on her own, and she was starting to enjoy the freedom that this would bring her. Riches beyond her wildest imagination.

"Stay focused. You're almost there," Catalina said to herself as she left the apartment and locked the door behind her.

THIRTY-ONE

Ignacio didn't know what was going on, or what he would do. Here he was with Diego and Rick on the way to possibly kill Catalina and get the treasure. It was his fault. If he hadn't told her about it, her life wouldn't be in danger.

But she went behind my back and stole what was rightfully mine, Ignacio thought. *What I would have shared with the entire crew. I wouldn't have told her if I knew how she really was. She was playing me this entire time.*

So why should he be worried about her? She deserved to die. Though, Ignacio knew deep down he didn't really mean those words. As much as he was able to keep control over his crew –until he got shot and was out of commission – he was never one for random violence, or even violence for petty things. He'd throw someone out for lying to him, leave them alone on the streets. Even ratting someone out, an offense punishable by death in most gangs, only warranted a beat down and shunning. An action worthy of death? He hadn't come across that yet in order to make a decision.

This came damn close, though. Catalina had shot a few arrows at him. He felt betrayed as a leader, but worse, betrayed in his heart. He thought she really liked him, and it turns out she was probably playing with his emotions just to get what she wanted.

Is this how all girls were? He hoped not. Miss JoJo didn't appear to be that way. Maybe once girls turned into women they stopped playing games. Ignacio had a lot to think about, but right now the treasure came first.

Diego's truck made quick work of the roads, saving themselves a lot of sweat and legwork just to walk a couple miles.

Diego slowed down as they rounded the corner and Cuba's destroyed house came into view, then cut the wheel and went off road, onto the beach.

"Where?" he asked as the wind and sand whipped up around them.

Ignacio pointed to the spot he'd long ago memorized, a sinking feeling in his gut.

Part of him had hoped that Catalina hadn't taken the treasure. It was the same part of him that now felt heavy with betrayal as they skidded out close to the waterline. He didn't see a chest peaking out above the water, and wouldn't at this time of day. But he didn't need to see it to confirm that they were going to be broken and empty. He felt it in his gut.

Diego flung himself out of the truck and made a beeline into the water. He kicked around, twisting and turning, then finally dunked under. A few seconds later, he came up sputtering and rubbing salt water out of his eyes.

"I don't see anything. You need to think really hard about what you say next, because I've about had it with all these false leads and fairy tales."

"It's farther. You can't walk to it yet. Once the tide goes out, you can. But there's nothing there. I can feel it. Catalina stabbed me in the back."

He felt a hand on his shoulder, and looked back to see Rick standing next to him.

"Where would she bring it? The treasure? If she came here and took it, then it would have been hidden somewhere." Rick looked between Diego and Ignacio.

Trying to calm down Diego, Ignacio thought.

A good move on Rick's part, but he was pretty sure that once Diego was amped up the only thing that would bring him down was a whole lot of vengeance. And the louder and bloodier it was, the better.

"She has a place. Someplace hidden. I don't know where it is. Only the girls in the crew know. It's kind of a tradition, having a secret girl's place to hang out. Kid's stuff, I guess."

"And you're saying in all the time this tradition has been happening, none of you boys ever followed one there to find out where it was?" Rick asked.

Ignacio shook his head. "No, sir. I don't think you understand just how sacred we take our traditions. To do this would be like you, I don't know, breaking one of the commandments. Like... uh, well I guess you already broke that one. Um, like–"

"Yeah I get your point, kid. What about you, Captain Cartel? Weren't you in this street gang back in the day? You never got curious and checked out this girl cave?" Rick asked Diego.

"Never. Like Ignacio said, it's tradition. And while I don't give a damn about tradition if it gets in the way of my goal, there is another reason why the boys are so hesitant to find it. The girls, they threaten to cut off our huevos. That would get in the way of many of my goals."

Diego ran his hand through his wet hair and looked around. He stared behind them and nodded.

"This close to that house and none of you thought of looking right here?" he asked.

"Sometimes it's harder when something is hidden in plain sight."

"Do you think he came back and emptied out whatever he could find? Cuba?"

"I think he freaked out when he saw it and went underground until he could gather himself together and get some loyal men with him."

"And then?"

"I don't know. Start a war? Pick us all off one by one, or send a bunch of men with a ton of ammo and raid your compound."

"What about the treasure? Do you think that's first on Cuba's list, or is it meant to be part of the spoils of his so-called war?"

"I don't know that guy well enough to answer that. We'd need Ernie here. Or Grace would be better."

Diego looked at Ignacio. He flinched at the stare, but held it. What was cold and icy dissolved into amusement.

"Let's go explore that abandoned shithole house, sound fun?"

Ignacio grinned and ran off ahead of them. He enjoyed going through someone else's stuff. It was rare when he had a chance to do it without having to worry if the owners were going to walk in on him.

"Wait." He heard a voice yell behind him.

"The structure is unstable," Rick said, coming up next to him. "Let me take point until we get through the rubble into the unburnt part."

"I think he'll take you, your girlfriend, and the others out first. Doesn't need more than one guy to do it. Get you out of the way and then deal with me. Or attempt to deal with me. It makes more sense that way." Diego followed Rick and Ignacio.

"Is that your professional opinion?"

Diego shrugged. "I have experience and intuition. It'd be a good idea to listen to what I say."

"Yeah, well I don't like what you're saying about me and JoJo getting taken out. Makes me think I should give you the slip, find her, and get the hell out of Mexico."

"You can do that, sure." Diego said. "Hell, I'll even let you walk now if you want. But I have a better idea. This is why I need to check the house. Stick around and I'll explain it when it makes sense. Or leave. Up to you."

Ignacio watched Diego take the lead and pick his way through the rubble. He looked at Rick, who seemed torn between decisions. He grabbed him by the arm and pulled him toward the house.

"Come on, Mr. Rick. Getting the hell out of Mexico will be a lot easier if you have Diego helping you out."

THIRTY-TWO

Cuba felt happy for the first time in weeks, maybe months. He stood in the courtyard of the resort and clapped his hands so everyone would stop talking and face him.

Like a small army, they all snapped to and stood at attention.

"At ease," Cuba said and chuckled. He was really enjoying this.

While the handful of tourists had long since rushed inside and away from the pool area, Cuba knew there might be eyes watching them. The staff was definitely monitoring the situation, and it wouldn't be long before the cartel's sicarios would be here to engage.

Cuba knew the first to arrive had already gone out to hunt for these people. Cuba hoped this was all for naught and Captain Jonah had already gotten his whale.

He smiled at his own joke, but saw several of the men glance at one another.

They probably think I'm insane, Cuba thought. *Good. It might keep them in line.*

"I trust you all know your assignment. I want to keep this focused and we need to do this in a timely manner, before all hell breaks loose," Cuba said.

He saw there were many questions on their faces. "Any questions?"

Nearly every hand went up.

Cuba pointed to the man closest to him.

"Obviously the cartel is a huge factor in all of this. Are the group we're being paid to take down with the cartel?"

"No," Cuba lied. It was better to keep these men in the dark. Not that it really mattered, because they'd be fighting off the cartel hitmen soon enough. "You might very well run into the sicarios, but that is not the focus. We're in Mexico, which means nothing moves without the corrupt government or the various cartels knowing about it."

"Hazard pay?" Another man asked.

Cuba smiled. "Of course. I've paid you all half upfront but the rest upon completion, as well as a sizable bonus." He didn't want to say *for those still alive*, but knew these men had already figured that out.

There were no more questions. Cuba wondered if that was because they already knew what they had to do and what was at stake, or if they didn't want to know anymore. Sometimes the mystery was good enough for men like this.

"Go. They need to be found and eliminated. I want no witnesses and I want no one still alive at the end of the day," Cuba said. Not that he thought they'd take care of all of his enemies within a day, but it sounded like the thing to say.

As one, they turned and were off.

Cuba knew they had more than enough firepower to get the job done.

The only way this will go south is if Diego and the damn cartel counters with their own group of men and firepower, Cuba thought.

He wanted to lounge near the pool and finish another bottle of rum but figured it wasn't safe. There might be snipers getting into position right now, ready to put a bullet through his head.

"Um, sir, do you have a second?" It was one of the managers of the resort, trying to block Cuba from entering back inside the building and the air conditioning. "We have guests who are saying—"

"Let them talk," Cuba said and took out his wad of cash, peeling off two hundred dollar bills slowly. "This should take care of it, right? Don't bother me anymore. In fact, here's another hundred. I'll need a few more bottles of rum. Got it?"

Cuba didn't wait for an answer, pushing past the man, who'd pocketed the cash.

Welcome to Mexico, where everyone has their hand in your pocket for a payout, Cuba thought. If he wasn't looking for the treasure and trying to kill everyone he'd worked with in his past, he might like it here.

Cuba figured he could buy a huge mansion up on a hill somewhere, overlooking his kingdom. The cartels would have to deal with him and he'd make sure they stayed clear of his wants and needs. They wanted to push drugs north and into the United States? So be it.

Money wasn't going to be an issue soon. In fact, Cuba knew he had most of Ernie Patek's offshore accounts at his disposal.

Which led him to think about why he was still in Mexico and why he cared about the treasure and any of these minor people that were no longer even in his life.

Cuba could live the rest of his life without having to work. He'd only cleared out a small portion of Ernie's bank accounts.

Why is Ernie still in this, too? He obviously has more money than he'll ever need. He's like me... it's all about the action, about the thrill of it. The money is just a small side benefit to what we're doing, Cuba thought.

He decided, if he was ever in the same room with a living, breathing Ernie Patek... he'd ask the man. Then he'd end his life.

Even though they'd been friends for a long time, partners in crime on numerous occasions, Cuba knew it was all about making money between them. That was the bottom line.

There was a knock at the door, which got Cuba up off of his chair with a Glock in hand. He hesitated, fearful if he said anything a hail of bullets would enter through the door and kill him.

"Sir, rum is being delivered, sir."

Cuba stood to the right of the door. "Thank you. Just leave it in the hallway."

"Uh... I'm not sure that's a good idea. There are many people walking about."

Cuba opened the door and let the man see the weapon in his hand. "Then hurry up and bring it inside."

The man had a large cardboard box of rum bottles, which he lifted and dragged inside, putting it on the table. He turned to Cuba and smiled.

"Thanks," Cuba said, waving with the gun for the man to leave.

When the man didn't move, Cuba groaned. "You people are incredible." He took out his wad of cash and handed the man a twenty dollar bill. "Now get out."

As soon as the man was out of the room, Cuba locked the door and dropped the Glock on his bed. He took a bottle of rum and opened it, taking a generous guzzle of it as he went to the window.

The curtains were drawn. He parted them with a finger and looked outside, but from this vantage point all he could see was bushes and the ocean in the distance.

"I hope they kill everyone quickly, because I'm going to be in trouble if they do not succeed," Cuba whispered to himself before taking another drink from the bottle of rum.

He couldn't remember the last time he'd slept. He knew as soon as his head hit the pillow he'd be out for hours.

Not yet. I need to stay awake and get updates from the team. I need to make sure this is going as planned, Cuba thought.

He took another sip of rum.

THIRTY-THREE

Captain Jonah didn't want to deliver the woman directly to Cuba. Not alive, at least. Cuba had been clear that he was supposed to kill the ones he found, not bring them back for a family reunion.

Jonah had no qualms with killing women. He'd done so in the past, and hoped he'd do it again in the future. After all, what fun would life be without being able to hunt down the weak stock in this world?

He just wasn't used to a quick kill. A drive-by. A wham, bam, see-you-in-hell-ma'am. He liked to play with his food. A kill wasn't as satisfying if the prey wasn't jacked full of adrenaline and fear. He needed to look into their eyes and see that knowledge that they were about to die, mixed with the terror of the unknown and a relief that what he had put them through was about to end.

Jonah also heard the release of all those chemicals before death made human flesh taste better. He wouldn't know, as he hadn't gotten up the courage to try it, but it was definitely on his bucket list.

He'd choked out JoJo, tied her up, and threw her in the back of his Jeep. She may be a little on the older side, but she was still one hell of a woman. Too good to waste with a bullet to the back of the head.

He would have his fun and Cuba would never know the difference. He'd just know that Jonah had successfully completed his mission. Game over. You win. Collect your cash and get out of Mexico.

He drove down the road to what remained of Cuba's old headquarters, now mostly rubble with parts still smoking. Cuba hadn't told him this was his old place, but Jonah did his homework before he flew in. The last thing most of the men Cuba was bringing in wanted to know was that the prior house had been bombed and gutted by the cartel. It wasn't a good look, so he was smart to keep that from them. But Jonah liked to know every detail about what he was walking into.

He also didn't care that the cartel was involved and had already made a move on Cuba. The more dangerous the enemy, the better the kill.

He parked in a small copse close by the house and dragged JoJo from the back. She was starting to come to, but still groggy enough to not have all her faculties up and running. He hadn't tied her legs because he needed her to walk with him into the burnt wreck to the wing that was still standing. Carrying her or dragging her would have been a nightmare. Something he learned from the last time he did this.

Jonah needed a place to play with his toys and, while he wouldn't have had an issue breaking into a house, killing the occupants, and taking it for his own, that would have opened up some possibilities for things to go wrong. A family member dropping by. A nosy neighbor. Jehovah's Witnesses. Using an abandoned building like this was a better idea.

By the time he got to the inside basement entrance, JoJo had started putting up more of a fight. He pulled his gun and pressed it against her temple.

"Don't make me be a cliche and warn you about all the things I'll do if you don't cooperate. Just do it." She stopped trying to kick him, but her breathing was still rapid and angry. "Good enough for now. Get moving."

Jonah pushed her toward the open door with the stairs leading down to the basement. They led down and underneath the rubble. He had checked it out before bringing the first one here and the ceiling appeared structurally stable. No fire had eaten through, and no debris had punched its way into the basement.

Better yet, there appeared to already be rings bolted into the wall. Judging by the opened and discarded handcuffs on the floor, Cuba had had at least a couple prisoners held captive down there in the past.

Jonah pushed JoJo down the last two stairs and grinned as she fell on her face and knees. That would leave a few good marks on her. The first of many to come.

He grabbed her by the hair and pushed her against the wall with the one remaining set of rings bolted into it. After handcuffing her to the rings, he grabbed an old stool from the corner and sat facing his two captives.

His favorite part was watching them wake up and realize that what they thought may have been a nightmare was reality.

The blonde was already awake and silent, staring at him with daggers in her eyes. Oh, the youth were always so confident that they would live forever.

JoJo stirred and her eyes seemed to clear up.

"Grace?" she asked, staring at her fellow captive.

"I guess this means you didn't get away. That makes two of us. Bastard grabbed me shortly after we left the beach. Didn't have a moment to try to find the kids and the –" Grace glance at Jonah, "– stuff."

"Don't worry, you two can talk freely in front of me. There's nothing I don't know about the treasure, about each of you."

"Do you know where the treasure is? Because nobody else seems to," JoJo asked.

"I do know where it is. It's in the ether. It's a mirage. It never existed. My current employer seems to have lost his head trying to find something that doesn't exist."

"Then why is he trying to kill us? If there's nothing for us to steal from him, then there's no reason to not let us go." Grace shifted, trying to get her feet underneath her.

"Tie up loose ends. I don't know. All I know is that, after seeing you two, I would have done this job for half the price. Maybe for nothing. The three of us are going to have a lot of fun together before I kill you."

JoJo and Grace started yelling and cursing at him. Jonah expected it, though usually it happened much sooner than this. The two women were tough, that was for sure. But he would break them down eventually. It didn't matter how hardened they were, they all broke over time.

Jonah grabbed a kitchen knife off the little tool desk and headed toward JoJo. He had already drawn blood from Grace. Now, it was the mature woman's time. Blood aged like fine wine.

Before he was able to make a nice slice across the side of her face, a thump came from above along with some dust and sediment falling from the ceiling.

Jonah took the roll of duct tape from his jacket pocket and covered both of their mouths before they could make more of a racket.

More thumping came from above. Footsteps.

What the hell? Jonah thought. *Who would be coming into this death trap now?*

He made his way slowly up the stairs, avoiding most of the creaking areas he had tried to remember. He cracked the door open just a little and put his ear to the opening.

Men in the house. No, wait. Two men, and what sounded like a kid.

Jonah smiled as they spoke to each other. Each name rang in his head like a dinner bell. This was going to be much easier than he thought.

THIRTY-FOUR

Within an hour or so they had all of the treasure secured in the warehouse. The group of street urchins had done well, but Catalina knew they were going to talk soon.

Already, they'd begun to whisper when they thought she wasn't listening. Some of them were starry-eyed, talking quietly about how they'd spend their share of the treasure. It was usually on stupid things, like a bicycle or a new stove for their mother.

Things anyone could buy.

Catalina was going to buy houses and airplanes and an army to protect her.

"We're all going to share in this wealth," Catalina said. "In time. I need everyone to sit here, against the wall. We need to talk. There are going to be rules. Understand?"

Everyone nodded and sat down against the wall.

Catalina stood over them, pacing back and forth and making sure to smile. "We are now all very wealthy, but there is a problem we must first solve."

She went to the door and threaded a chain through the handles, putting a lock onto it and pocketing the key.

All of the boys and girls simply watched her, which she was thankful for. If they started to question her this soon, she knew her plan would fail.

Catalina went back to the group, keeping the smile up despite her nerves nearly getting the best of her. "I need two volunteers."

Many hands were raised but she picked the two smallest children and handed them a long length of rope.

"What are we doing with this?"

Catalina waved her hand. "We're all going to spend the next day and night here. Together. While we figure out the best way to get this treasure out of town, along with our families. The cartel will be looking for it and maybe for us, so we need to be sure no one runs off and tells anyone before we're in agreement on a good plan of action. Does everyone understand so far?"

Most of them nodded but she saw a few giving glances to the others, ready to jump up and maybe run. Catalina didn't want to use force, not yet, but she would do what needed to be done.

I've already stepped over the line, Catalina thought.

"We're going to tie ourselves to one another, so no one leaves. In the morning we'll untie each other and do whatever we've discussed today. Simple and fair. Everyone will get a say and we'll all get an equal share." Catalina motioned for the kids with the ropes to begin tying everyone up.

"What about food?"

Catalina nodded. "I've got food and drink already lined up for us. It should be here in about an hour." It was a lie but that wasn't the worst thing that was coming to the crew.

She felt bad, a pit in her stomach. They had all been friends for so long, since they'd all met on the streets and began working together. It was a meager living and they'd barely been able to collectively support themselves or their families, and now, with a vast treasure in front of them...

Life is shit. Never fair. They should all remember that, Catalina thought.

She watched as the kids began to be tied together, a long line of them on the floor.

"What do we need to discuss? We split up the treasure equally and we go our separate ways," one of the kids said.

"Not so easy. There's too much for one person to carry and not be noticed." Catalina waved her hand at the wheelbarrows and boxes overflowing. "We need a better plan so that when it's time to leave and go our separate ways, no one will see what we actually have. Got it?"

"Then what do we do?"

Catalina sighed. "We figure out a good way to do it. Obviously."

She already had a couple of ideas but they would never work if she did it on her own. And yet, she couldn't take the chance of these kids keeping their mouths shut.

"Where are Ignacio and Arturo? They would know what to do."

"Hopefully they'll arrive at some point tonight, and then we'll tie them with us and we can work this out." Catalina wanted the kids to hurry up and finish tying the group together. It would make it easier for what she had to do.

"What about you? We're all tied together."

Catalina nodded. "Of course. Just one quick thing." She went to the desk and pulled open the drawer, taking out the Glock and the extra clip she had in the back.

Everyone's eyes went wide but no one said anything, not at first understanding what was happening. What was about to happen.

Catalina knew she was going to Hell for doing this, but she felt she had no choice.

"Straight to Hell, I'm going," Catalina said under her breath as she stepped forward and began shooting. She hoped the noise wouldn't draw nosy people. Most townsfolk knew better than to investigate gunshots.

Catalina knew if anyone decided to check it out, they couldn't easily get inside the warehouse. If they did she was sure she'd have extra ammo to take care of herself.

One by one the kids died by her hand. They tried to flee but were dragging one another with them, including the dead. There was nowhere to go, nowhere safe.

It was over quickly. Catalina still had ammo left, too.

She decided Ignacio was not going to get a cut of the treasure. He'd been stupid enough to tell her about it and to show her the spot. It was his own fault.

Catalina wondered if one of the bullets left would be for Ignacio. Better him than her, she decided.

She was exhausted. She sat down on the desk and fought back tears. How many had she killed in the past few days? Catalina had lost count. She knew she wasn't done, either.

Now, how to get rid of the treasure? Catalina wondered if she could keep the warehouse for a few weeks or months. The bodies would be a big problem, though. The smell would be too much, even for townsfolk who try to stay clear of trouble.

No, she'd need to bury them. All of them. That would take many hours, and it would be backbreaking work. Catalina wondered if she was up for it.

It's worth it if I can leave the country with the treasure, Catalina thought.

She wondered how she would do it, though. At her age, without her mother to help her... could she get a passport, a plane ticket, a way out?

Catalina had a lot to think about tonight.

Her worry was someone would realize what had happened and come looking for her. What if her mother had already been found? What if Ignacio had told the cartel about the treasure, and now they knew it was gone?

Catalina tried to shut her eyes to keep the tears from flowing, but it was no use.

She began to shake and put her head down on the desk, banging her fists on the wood in frustration.

"What am I going to do now?" Catalina asked.

THIRTY-FIVE

"What are we still doing here?" Baker asked.

"I told you already. We're planning," Ernie said, taking another bite of his burger.

Since it appeared that everybody had left except for the two of them and some guards, the kitchen was free game. No more Diego dictating what they could and couldn't eat, like the Devil himself.

"You keep saying that, but we've been sitting here doing nothing. Saying nothing. You think they'll let us walk out the front door like everybody else?"

"I don't know if there was ever a treat once that kid showed up. I'm just shocked he left us alive once the kid made us irrelevant. I mean, made you irrelevant. I always have chips to play," Ernie said.

"You need to stop saying that. Putting me down like that. I'm more useful than you realize, Patek. Just because we've become unlikely friends, doesn't mean you can bust my chops."

Ernie stopped eating and looked at Baker. There was a time when he would have avoided Ernie's gaze, but after everything they had been through, Baker realized that Ernie was a lot of talk, but little action. At least, he didn't personally get involved in the physical aspects of maintaining a criminal empire.

He was a dangerous man, but only when he had people around him to do his bidding.

"Nobody said we were friends, Baker. Don't assume things. Just because we've been through some shit together and happen to share some passions, like eating, doesn't make you a friend of mine. You know what it would do to my reputation if people found out I was friends with a DEA agent? And not friends because I was getting information, but friends like to hang out and watch the game, or go get a coffee?"

Baker felt a little hurt by Ernie's words, which surprised him. He never expected to like the guy. Patek always came off as a scumbag. But he had to admit that he had grown on him. And now Ernie was sabotaging whatever relationship they had built. Baker felt like he was sitting through a breakup conversation.

"Well, even if we're not, you still don't have the right to make me feel bad about myself. You couldn't have gotten here without me. You would have probably been killed in Mexico City."

"I'm not making you feel bad. You're making yourself feel bad. That's your choice. You wanna go, then go. It would probably be better for you anyway. Get out of here and get out of Mexico. Go back to your wife before you can't go back anymore."

Baker grabbed another burger and sat. He didn't want to leave. Not yet. He wasn't sure if they were any closer to getting at the treasure, or if there even was anything to find. But he was too deep in this to leave now. He'd rather his wife pass away not finding out that he was such a loser and wasn't able to get her better treatment and take care of her. He needed to find out one way or another what they were dealing with. Sunken treasure? A legend? He couldn't leave before then. If it was nothing, then at least he had tried. But if he left and found out later that it had been found, he'd probably take the next trip out of this life after his wife.

"No, we're in this together and I'm sticking it out. If you don't want to be friends, we can at least be temporary partners. Your street cred is fine if you're working with an agent doing something illegal."

Baker bit into the burger. It wasn't the best. The only ground meat in the fridge had already been seasoned with a bunch of spices. Probably for some kind of Mexican dish. But a burger was a burger, and enough ketchup covered up most of the potent ingredients.

"You talk to Grace again? See where's she at?"

"How would I talk to Grace?"

"On that app thingy you use. If I make it through this unscathed and with my reputation still intact, I really need to tell the agency about that. Imagine something on an app store being better than anything they have?"

"She can't initiate contact. Only I can do that. Though now that she knows those weren't just pretty earrings, I think there's a setting to turn that on. It doesn't matter right now. No, I haven't talked to her."

Ernie unlocked his phone and brought up the app. He hit a couple buttons and turned the volume up and on speaker.

It took Baker a minute to figure out what was going on. At first he thought they had dropped in on some casual conversation with Grace and some guy. But it quickly became clear whoever this guy was, he was holding Grace against her will. Then he heard JoJo's voice and looked up at Ernie in shock.

"Someone's got both of them," Baker said.

"Do you think so?" Ernie replied, rolling his eyes.

The conversation ended and it sounded like the guy left the room.

"Grace?" Ernie said into his phone. "Can you hear me or did you take off your earrings simply because I told you to keep them on and you like busting my balls?"

There was some muffled sound, shifting around, and a clinking that reminded Baker of tools rattling around in a trunk.

"Ernie," Grace said, her voice low, "as much as it pains me to say it, I need your help."

"What was all that noise?"

"I'm cuffed to some rings in the basement of Cuba's old place. Idiot put duct tape on my mouth, but all I had to do was lift myself up to my hands and take it off. Where are you?"

"Still at Diego's house. They left, though. Actually, Baker go get a guard and tell him we need to get a hold of Diego now. Grace, he's got to be somewhere near you. I'm going to try to get him to help you out. Kill that sonofabitch who took you."

Baker left the conversation and went out the side door of the kitchen. He almost bumped right into the guard standing outside. The man pushed him back and lifted his assault rifle just enough to show Baker he would have no problem shooting him in the face.

"Back inside."

"We need to get a hold of Diego. It's an emergency. If you don't want to use your cell, just let me know his number."

"Inside, now."

"Listen, it's important. What if I give you a dickfor?"

The guard frowned. "What's a dickfor?"

Baker kneed the man in his nuts and grabbed the rifle as he fell. He hadn't consciously planned to do it. Something about the conversation with Ernie calling him useless must have set something off inside of him.

He reared back and knocked the guard out with the butt of the rifle. Then hit him a couple more times just for good measure. He grabbed the man's cell and turned around only to run into Ernie.

"What the hell are you messing around out here for? It's time to go."

"But I... the guard... kicked his ass... gun," Baker said.

"Good bring the gun. I don't need Diego. I can rescue my daughter myself."

"You mean Cuba's daughter?"

Ernie took the gun from Baker and cleared it.

"No, I mean Grace. My daughter. It's time I showed up for her."

THIRTY-SIX

Maria had found out where Catalina lived, but all she found there was the girl's dead mother.

Where did this street rat go? She must have the treasure. She also likely had help from the others on the street, Maria thought.

The next place she checked was the old clubhouse, which looked like it was still in use. Maria actually stopped and looked around, smiling because she had so many great memories here.

The building was empty, which meant all of the street kids were out doing something else, which usually didn't fly. There had to be someone at the home base at all times to coordinate whatever was happening on the street.

Maria thought things had changed and only recently, and she had a good idea what it was.

Catalina had the treasure and she was hiding it, Maria thought. The alternative was she'd already started to move it, which would not be good.

It was highly unlikely she'd been able to get it out of town, let alone Mexico.

Maria kept on with her search, checking a couple of the old haunts only the girls knew about. They were empty but she saw they were still in use.

Curiously, there were no children on the streets. Usually at the corners of the main thoroughfares, one or two kids would be in sight, keeping an eye on things.

Maria saw no children. That meant they were all now working with Catalina, and it also meant there would be too many people who knew about the treasure.

I have no hesitation when it comes to killing, even children. I've done it before and I will surely do it again. I just need to find the girl and see if she has stolen the loot, Maria thought.

Maria knew her being on the street was a bad thing, because the cartel would know she was out and about. If Diego had said anything about her to the bosses back in Colombia, she could be a target.

I'll deal with that soon enough, she thought and kept going, trying to slip into alleys and side streets whenever possible.

There was a definite tension she could feel as she moved through the town. It was thick. There wasn't much talking and everyone seemed to be looking over their shoulder or had their head down.

Two SUVs drove past and Maria saw they were armed men, likely sicario. At least ten of them, all looking out the window as they drove by slowly.

Maria knew that meant there was an opposing force in town, too. Diego had his own men to do his bidding, and wouldn't ask for help unless he absolutely needed it.

Now she wondered if Diego had asked for more men or if something even bigger was happening.

Maria got part of the answer a couple of blocks away, when a carload of obvious American soldier-types drove fast down the street, nearly hitting a couple of townsfolk. They were hunting for someone or something, and Maria had no doubt she was on their list. If they saw her they would have stopped and perhaps even opened fire. Stupid American soldiers didn't waste time with words, they pulled the trigger.

The same with the cartel hitmen.

She wondered – and worried – there would be a war in the streets. That would not be a good look for the townsfolk, for Mexico or for the cartel.

At the next street she saw one of the other spots the girls would sometimes use, an old warehouse. When Maria tried the side door, she found it was locked. It only took her a few seconds to pick it, but the door wouldn't open.

It's barred from inside, which is a good sign. It means there is something important in there, Maria thought.

She slipped through the tight alley between the buildings and came to another door, one hardly anyone knew about. Back in her day, Maria had made sure this door was hidden from everyone, even the other girls. It had likely not been used in a dozen years or more, but Maria knew it would open quietly.

Maria had made sure to oil the new hinges when she'd been in the crew, and she smiled as she pushed open the door and it didn't make a noise.

Some things do last, she thought.

Inside she saw the door had been blocked by the false wall, which was still standing. She pushed it aside and stepped into the warehouse.

The first thing she noticed was the smell of spilt blood and saw the bodies.

It looked like the street crew had been tied up and killed.

Maria searched the bodies, trying to keep her distance, but she wasn't sure if Catalina was one of the females that was dead.

"She's not. She's the killer," Maria whispered. It was obvious, because there were wheelbarrows and storage tubs filled with gold and silver coins, crowns and jewels.

Maria had the urge to begin moving all of the treasure out the secret door and back to the villa, but knew that wouldn't work. Diego would take it and likely kill everyone.

There were too many well-armed men on the streets right now, too.

She also knew she couldn't trust the townspeople, her people, if they knew what she had.

Catalina had taken a huge risk moving it to the warehouse, and Maria knew she'd enlisted the crew to do it with her, and then wiped them out when they were no longer needed.

She'd also killed her own mother, which meant the girl wasn't much for sharing.

Not that she'd be able to get any of this out of Mexico, if that was her goal, Maria thought.

Catalina would need the help of the cartel, but Diego would simply shoot the girl in the head and take it all for himself.

Maria sat down at the desk and opened the drawers, smiling because there was a Glock, probably the one she'd put there, as well as ammo for the weapon.

"Some things never change," Maria thought.

The main door was padlocked and chained, which meant Catalina knew about the secret entrance. Which meant the girl would return soon enough and use it.

Maria wondered how to proceed. None of the men would know about the warehouse, so she didn't need to worry about being interrupted.

She was going to have a talk with Catalina and figure out the next course of action.

There are things set in motion that I need to work, Maria thought.

She left the Glock in the drawer but took all of the ammo, putting it in her pocket.

If Catalina was smart, she'd figure out a way to get to the desk and try to use the weapon on Maria, because that's what Maria would've done back in the day.

Maria paced around the warehouse, smiling because she could see some of the graffiti she had added to the walls when she was a teenager, and remembered some of her fallen crew members. The females that had given their life to the cause, and the ones that had checked out and gotten out of the life.

Ran off and got married, had children and jobs and a normal life.

Maria knew this was as normal as it would ever get for her.

THIRTY-SEVEN

After Grace confronted him on the beach with proof of the treasure Alberto's thoughts of taking off and disappearing into the horizon with the boat were squashed. He still thought that would be the best idea, but when the gold piece was flashed in front of his eyes, correct choices took second place to gold-colored possibilities.

Grace hadn't been back, or at least in contact since she'd left which concerned him. There were too many bad people looking for this treasure, and if someone found out she had a lead on it they could have done something with her. Took her and made her talk, give up names, locations. Or Cuba could have grabbed her again, found the coin, and was now raking up the rest of it and leaving Alberto out of the grab.

There was only one way to find out, or at least to rule out Cuba having Grace. Alberto knew Cuba, in the kind of way you really could know someone who had forced you to do things against your will. The rest? These cartel people. Ernie Patek. He only knew enough to stay away if at all possible.

He could also just be overthinking things. Grace was a young, but grown woman and she definitely had an I'll-do-what-I-want attitude. He didn't think she'd make the effort to come see him and tip him off and then just screw him over. But he did think that maybe, if she wasn't in trouble, she was getting the wheels in motion to recover the treasure without tipping off Cuba or the cartel.

Alberto slipped the biometric lock around the steering wheel and pressed his thumb against it to confirm it was closed. The problem with boats is that you couldn't lock the doors like a car. Thieves could hop on, hotwire it, and drive away within a minute. The only option was to lock the wheel. There may be better ways of securing a boat, but whatever they were, Alberto was sure he didn't have the money to do it. At least, not yet.

Alberto walked. His car, even with the four doors and alarm system, had been stolen long ago, and in this small town it made no sense to break the bank to buy another one.

The good thing was that Cuba's new place wasn't too far of a hike from the boat dock. In fact, both of the places Cuba had since Alberto had been unfortunate enough to meet him, were along the same strip of sand, about a mile or so away and not too far from each other.

He went up the hill into the edges of town since he couldn't walk the beach the entire way. There were too many areas of thick jungle cutting into the sand, and he had no desire to trek his way through there. It was a good way to come face-to-face with a snake, and he was already on the way to see the king of the snakes.

Something struck him as strange as he passed the squat buildings and open businesses. He couldn't immediately place it until he saw a mother with her two young children walking out of a clothing store.

No street rats. Where the hell did they all go? Alberto thought.

They were usually spread out around town, a tactic used to better increase their chances of picking pockets, or getting more money begging in front of the more upscale stores that had recently started popping up around town as the tourist industry increased.

And there were always a handful of them in this area.

Usually, Alberto wouldn't give it more than a passing thought, but since Ignacio was in the hands of the cartel, he wondered if maybe the kid had said or done something that either got the other rats rounded up, or put them on notice to not be so vulnerable on the streets until things blew over.

A little further down, a couple Jeeps were parked down a side road. Men in civilian clothes with automatic weapons stood around the cars, checking themselves and having what seemed like casual conversation. Whatever they were doing there, it was an obvious meet-up zone. A place to get things settled before heading to the main event.

Although he didn't want to be right, Alberto was pretty sure he knew where that was going to be. He was just surprised the cartel had decided to take the offensive instead of waiting for Cuba and his men to come to them and have the home-field advantage.

A couple of the men turned to look at him and Alberto shifted his gaze, trying to look like a normal guy taking a stroll along the beach walk like he didn't have a care in the world.

Once they were out of sight, he picked up the pace. While he was no fan of Cuba, the cartel had been a bigger issue with him in the past. He wouldn't mind seeing that entire crew neutralized.

Cuba's old place came into view as he turned the corner. A giant wreck, mostly a husk from the fire. What was still standing was tilting a little too much to the right. It gave him vertigo just looking at its odd angle.

He couldn't believe that just a short time ago they were all pinned inside that house, let out only at Cuba's whim. It felt like years. He couldn't remember how long it had been since he'd seen Rick or JoJo. He remembered the situation of their last meetings, but time was lost to him.

A noise came from the house, like rocks dropping or books falling off shelves. For a moment, Alberto thought the remaining standing wing was about to finally tip and collapse.

Then the voices came.

They were muffled and low in volume. If cars had been driving by he would never have heard anything.

It sounded like an argument inside, more than two people yelling at each other. And considering the history of the house, whatever was going inside couldn't be good. The only people found in a half burnt dwelling were people who, at best, were up to no good and, at worst, were planning extreme violence.

Alberto, against his better judgment (he was beginning to question whether he had good instincts at all), headed to the collapsed entrance of the house, grabbing a hefty rock along the way.

Whatever was going on inside had something to do with the craziness his life had been since he'd been brought on to captain the boat. He'd lost everything since then, so what was on the line now except his life?

When he made it through the maze of collapsed wood and stone, he was able to peek through a section of crumbled sheetrock and saw Rick and Ignacio, along with Diego. They were all arguing with someone he couldn't see. Diego had a handgun, but it was at his side, not pointed forward. Which meant that whoever the out of sight man was, he had the advantage.

They backed up to the far wall, and a tall, muscled man came into view with a large weapon pointed at them. And, like all men with big guns and a perceived advantage, he talked way too much.

Alberto caught enough of the conversation to realize that Grace and JoJo were captive in the basement, and this mercenary was bragging about killing all of them.

He should just leave. It wasn't being a coward. What could he do, one man against what was obviously a trained killing machine?

Something snapped behind him and Alberto's bladder almost let go. Then, a hand grabbed his shoulder and another covered his mouth.

"Don't yell and don't freak out. What's that smell? Did you make a little pee-pee in your pants?"

Alberto's tension left his body as he recognized the voice behind him.

He turned to see Ernie and Baker, weaponized and with a fire in their eyes he never noticed before.

Now things were getting interesting.

THIRTY-EIGHT

Catalina wanted to kick herself for being so stupid, acting like she was smarter than everyone else.

I'm dumb. That's the only excuse I have, she thought.

Now that she thought about it, the back door had been opened further than she'd remembered the last time she'd used it. That should've been the sign to not enter, to go and find a weapon and watch the warehouse for a few hours until she was sure no one was inside.

Catalina had walked right into the warehouse, into what she now saw as a trap, and had gone halfway across the warehouse floor when she'd seen the woman leaning against the wheelbarrows, smiling.

"Ahh, Catalina, right? I see you've been busy." Maria, Ignacio's aunt and a leader of the cartel, seemed relaxed.

And why shouldn't she be? She'd figured out how to get into the warehouse and had obviously found all the treasure.

"Ma'am," Catalina said respectfully. She angled toward the desk, hoping that the woman hadn't been here long enough to check for the Glock.

"I see the girls still use this warehouse," Maria said. She didn't have a weapon in hand, but Catalina knew there was one within easy reach.

Catalina shook her head. "Only I use it now."

Maria glanced at the dead children against the wall. "Yeah, I guess so."

"No, even before... before this. An older girl showed this to me many years ago, but I chose not to share it with the others. I knew, some day, I would need it for myself," Catalina said.

Maria nodded. "For when you screw everyone over, especially Ignacio, and steal all of the treasure for yourself. I have to hand it to you, Catalina... you've done a lot of work. I am genuinely impressed with your skills. It reminds me of me at your age."

"I did what had to be done for my family." Catalina kept moving, casually aiming for the desk. If she were lucky, Maria wouldn't even think about what Catalina was doing.

"Your family?" Maria shook her head. "I saw your mother. What was left of her, anyway. That's no way to treat family, Catalina. Has this wealth blinded you to the truth?"

Catalina smiled. "Are you going to tell me what the truth is now, ma'am? You of all people?"

"What's that supposed to mean?" Maria was no longer smiling but she hadn't drawn a weapon, which Catalina took to be a good sign.

Catalina got to the desk and put a hand on the chair, as if she were simply going to have a seat. ""I know about you and Ignacio. It seems like he was the only one who didn't know."

"And what about it? I had to protect my son. One day, if you survive that long, you'll have to make decisions about a child.

Hopefully you won't give birth to a monster like yourself, who will end up killing you because of their greed," Maria said.

Catalina sat down in the chair and pulled open the drawer with a smile, Glock now in hand and aimed at Maria. "I'm done talking to you."

Maria chuckled. "Oh, are you? Are you going to shoot me like you did all of your crew? There is no loyalty with you. Have you ever heard the expression *no honor among thieves*? That is you."

Catalina pulled the trigger. She was done talking to this woman. Catalina knew she had things to do, plans to put into motion, and some old woman wasn't going to stand in her way.

The gun clicked, several times, but Maria was still alive.

"The Glock in your hand? It was mine. Many years ago. An old lover gave it to me, showed me how to use it. How to kill with it. When he put a baby in me, Ignacio, he decided he didn't want to be a father to a child. Not that young. Not with all the power he saw before him. He's done quite well for himself, and so have I," Maria said. "I fear that you think too highly of yourself, Catalina. That will get you into real trouble. It will get you buried and forgotten."

Catalina dropped the Glock onto the desk. "Now what? Are you going to pull out your new Glock and shoot me? Go ahead already. I'm not afraid to die."

Maria laughed. "Not afraid to die? Then you are even dumber than I first thought."

"I live my life like there's no tomorrow," Catalina said simply.

"And yet, you've taken the steps to secure your future, or what you hope it will be," Maria said. "So you are obviously thinking about tomorrow."

"Maybe. Maybe for the first time ever. Getting out of this town. Starting a new life somewhere else, like in California or Greece or... I don't really know." Catalina glanced at the unloaded Glock again. "Anywhere but here, no?"

"I agree. I got out."

Catalina smiled. "And yet... here you are."

Maria shrugged. "Sometimes you have to come home in order to fully get away from it."

"That makes no sense," Catalina said.

Maria shrugged again. "Someday it will make sense. When I was your age it made no sense to me, either. None of this did. I wasn't thinking about the next day or the next. Living solely in the moment. Wondering if I'd ever catch a break. If my life was going to be living in the structure or a children's street gang and then moving up to a teenage gang and then to the cartel and nothing more."

"And here you are." Catalina waved her hand at Maria. "Head of a cartel. Impressive. The dream every girl on the street has."

Maria glanced at the bodies against the wall again. "Are there any girls left on the street these days?"

"There will be. You grew up in this town so you know that every teenage girl has a better than average chance of getting pregnant. I might've wiped out the crew but someone else will step in and fill the vacuum." Catalina stood. "Are you going to shoot me? I'm done talking."

Maria slowly withdrew a Glock from the back of her waistband but didn't aim it at Catalina. "Do you want me to shoot you, Catalina?"

"No. I'd rather you took a handful of gold coins and left through the back door to leave me alone with my riches," Catalina said.

"I'm sure you do." Maria still hadn't aimed the Glock at Catalina. "Well, that isn't going to happen."

"Then what is going to happen?"

Maria glanced at the bodies again. "It would seem to be such a waste if I killed you. Added you to the pile. No, I have a deal for you. If you take it you work for me and you live another day. If you say no..." Maria shrugged her shoulders.

"Then I imagine I need to say yes, to whatever you need me to do," Catalina said.

"Exactly. This treasure is now mine. The warehouse as well. I'm going to need you to either drag the bodies out back and bury them or figure out a way to mask the smell." Maria put the Glock away. "It doesn't bother me. I've been around plenty of the dead, but it might attract unwanted attention."

"The dead don't bother me, either," Catalina said.

THIRTY-NINE

There were too many people around him. Cuba had handled large groups of mercenaries before, and with great success. But he'd never had them all coming and going from the place where he lived. And this current hotel was even smaller than the last one.

It felt almost claustrophobic, and he couldn't seem to get a moment to himself to try to gather his thoughts.

"Everyone is now here and accounted for," the soldier Cuba had appointed second-in-command said. "Should we get everyone inside? Isn't going to look good with all those men and guns hanging around if a cop car rolls by."

"The cops here are on the cartel's dole. They don't do anything unless they are told to. And I have a feeling they've been told to close their eyes for the next couple days."

"So what's the plan? What next?"

Cuba groaned and poured himself a drink. The problem with these people is that they were too eager to get to the next thing. It used to be that you shut your mouth until you were told what to do, not try to learn the plan all up front.

It would have been easier on Cuba if it was like that, since whatever plan he had was still forming in his head. Sure, he knew he was going to come head-to-head with the cartel in these parts at some point soon, but he hadn't yet figured out how to approach that.

Should he battle it out on the streets of this town, no regard for the people who lived here, until the last man standing won? Or should he be a bit more strategic?

The people the cartel were sending knew how to fight between buildings and down alleys, through patches of jungle. And this was their home turf. It seemed smarter to come at them in a way they weren't used to. Throw them off their game. At least shake things up enough to give himself better odds.

If you let the enemy dictate the terms, the land, and the methods, you were dead before the fighting even started.

"What's next is you go stand your post until I tell you otherwise. Any news from town?"

"One of the men radioed in. He was sitting at the cafe watching, pretending to be a tourist as you told him to. A group of men in a Jeep drove by. Armed. Another group drove through shortly afterward."

"So they're massing in the town, but haven't moved on us here yet. That's good. They're either waiting for the go ahead, or have been told to hold off and wait for us to make the first move. Either way, it's something we can take advantage of."

"And then?"

"And then, what?"

"We take them out. Everything's great for the moment. But the cartel is just going to send in more people. More guns. Until we give up or we die."

"We'll have time. This isn't sanctioned. It's one man with a big head using his cartel resources for his own personal gain. If, by some chance, he beats us and is standing over my dying body, my last breath will be a happy one. Because Diego Santiago dies by our hand, or by his own cartel's hands."

"Never going to happen. We'll take these guys down like it's nothing."

"Watch the confidence. Too much and you can make mistakes. Now get the men organized and let me figure out the next move."

The man left and Cuba poured himself another drink. It probably wasn't the best idea to get a good buzz going when the Mexican mob was coming after you. But, then again, who wanted to go into a firefight sober?

He pulled out his phone and dialed. A few rings later, Jonah answered.

"What took you so long?" Cuba asked.

"Ran into a little complication. Well, maybe not so much a complication as a bit of luck."

"What do you mean? And what's happening with tracking down those people?"

"I got two. Two of the women. No idea where the Mexican whore is, but I'll find her. But it seems like some of them are finding me. I have a gun pointed at Rick, Diego, and that kid Taco."

Cuba heard the kid yell 'Ignacio' in the background.

"What do you mean, they found you?"

"I have JoJo and Grace chained up in your old place. These three happened to walk in. So like I said, a lucky complication."

"I told you that your job is to execute them. A bullet to the head. Simple and over in a second. Not to play with them like they're your personal toys. And especially not Grace. She's to be taken care of as painlessly as possible."

"Whatever you say, boss. These three will be dead the second you hang up."

"And the two girls. I know the stories about you. No fucking around."

"Me? I would never do that."

"Wait a minute," Cuba said. He emptied the rest of his glass. "I want Diego alive. Kill the rest, and bring him to me. Right now, he's more useful if he's breathing."

"Got it. Over and out."

The connection clicked off and Cuba stared at the screen. He knew Captain Jonah would be a possible problem, a loose cannon, but he was top dog in what he did. The man was a lunatic, though. Cuba would have to make sure to cut him loose as soon as he was done killing the rest of them. He didn't want him involved in the cartel fight. The guy would probably wind up taking out just as many men with friendly fire as he would the enemy.

This entire Mexican thing had been a mess from the beginning. And the treasure was a joke at this point. Cuba wondered if maybe Ernie had masterminded the entire thing just to push him into chaos. He did have a daughter with Ernie's wife. That alone would be enough of a reason to try to take him down.

But Patek wasn't smart enough to plan out something so extravagant. Neither did he have the patience for such an extended con. He would have just had Cuba killed and be done with it.

He was beginning to accept that the treasure, if it existed, was a lost cause. It was upsetting, considering how much time he had put into finding it. But live and learn. There will be more treasure in the future, in one form or another.

Right now, his main focus was the cartel men. Cuba was almost positive that Diego hadn't passed on any information about him or what he was doing to his superiors. This was strictly a cash grab, and Diego was too greedy to share any of it. Cuba figured if he could take down these men who were building up in town, then silence Diego, he wouldn't be looking over his shoulder for the rest of his life, waiting for a sicario to get revenge.

If he did wind up being a target of the cartels, then so be it. They would have to get in line with a whole bunch of other pissed off people.

The important thing was getting his men engaged with Diego's men. That would cause more than enough of a distraction. Because, despite his men thinking he was going to be leading them into battle, Cuba was ready to sneak out of Mexico while the sound of gunshots was still in the air.

FORTY

Baker felt exposed, but Ernie didn't seem to care. They were inside the remains of the villa, moving slowly.

Voices, muffled, from down below. Quite a few, in fact.

Baker tapped Ernie on the shoulder and leaned close. "What are we doing?"

"I'm going to rescue my daughter." Ernie had a Glock in his hand. Baker wondered if the big man actually knew how to use it. A guy like Patek usually paid other people to do the dirty work, like rescuing family members and shooting guns.

Baker wondered who he was trying to kid himself. When was the last time he'd shot a weapon, except to qualify to carry it? He'd never come close to pulling his weapon on the job.

Once, he'd accidentally dropped his weapon when he was trying to get out of his vehicle and his shoulder holster had caught on the seat belt strap. Luckily, it hadn't been discharged or he would've had to file a report and answer for it.

Ernie stopped walking and turned slowly in a circle.

"What's the matter?" Baker asked.

"I don't know where they are. I think I hear Grace," Ernie said quietly. He pointed his weapon down at the debris-strewn floor. "Downstairs, right? There had to be an elevator."

Baker sighed. "Why would an elevator work in this villa? It's been destroyed. Stairs. We need to find the damn stairs."

"There were stairs? Really? Interesting," Ernie said quietly.

Baker shook his head and started to walk, careful where he stepped. Even though he could still hear talking from below, if they tripped over debris or kicked something across the room it would alert whoever was down there.

He knew Grace would be here and in trouble. That's why they'd shown up, not even bothering to think this through.

Baker stopped and watched Ernie walk past him.

"Come on, what are you waiting for?" Ernie asked. "Find the stairs, if there really are any."

"I can't do this," Baker said. The thought had struck him like a bolt of lightning. He shouldn't be here, he should be back home with his wife. His sick wife, who might not even be alive at this point.

Ernie either didn't hear the comment or he ignored it, continuing to shuffle along.

"I'm going home," Baker said. "I'm sorry."

Ernie turned back and frowned. "You're joking, right? Please tell me you're having a laugh."

Baker shook his head. "My wife needs me."

"Your wife needs a lot of money for medical bills and to live the rest of her life, even if it's short," Ernie said. "Nothing personal, but you did say she was really sick."

"I made a huge mistake coming here." Baker knew he needed to get out of Mexico and go home. He also knew he'd likely be detained as soon as he landed in a United States airport.

"You came for the fabulous wealth we're all going to have." Ernie shrugged. "I mean, the ones who are left standing at the end. We're close. I can feel it. Stay with me, Baker. I... could use your help right now."

"Right now? And then what? I've been on the sidelines for most of this. All of it, in fact. What's my contribution, huh?" Baker shook his head. He took a step away but then turned back, his body and mind fighting. The smart move was to leave. There wasn't a treasure, there was never going to be one found, and even if it actually existed – and Baker had a lot of doubts – he'd be killed before he got to touch it.

"I need to see my wife." Baker turned to walk away.

"So, that's it? You're a quitter? I thought you were an FBI agent," Ernie said.

Baker shook his head and turned back. "DEA. Motherfucker, I'm DEA." He tried to calm down because he was raising his voice, which was not good. "I am a quitter, okay? I quit everything and everyone. I ran away because I couldn't see my wife like that. I know that now. I'm a chickenshit and scared."

Ernie smiled. "I need you. Don't quit on me. Of all people. We have a bond, Baker. We're going to come out the other end of this and be very rich. You have to trust me."

Baker knew he couldn't trust Ernie Patek. He'd never been able to, he'd never be able to. The man was utter chaos.

"Help me save Grace. We're wasting precious time," Ernie said. He looked like he was trying puppy eyes or something equally weird.

"What are you doing with your face?" Baker asked.

Ernie kept doing it. "I'm showing you my sad face, so you will come to your senses and help me."

"Stop doing that. You look creepy."

"Then help me." Ernie swung his arm the way they'd been headed. "We have stairs to find and damsels in distress to save."

Baker thought that was funny. "I doubt anyone would ever call Grace a damsel in distress. A damsel who is a mess? Yep. I can see that."

"I want Grace to meet your wife," Ernie said.

That nearly broke Baker for some reason. He knew Patek was lying through his teeth. He couldn't care less about Baker or his wife, but he was pulling on heartstrings and it might be working.

"I can't..." Baker sighed.

The talking below had stopped for a few seconds, and Baker put up his hand.

Ernie opened his mouth to speak but Baker waved at him and put a finger to his lips. That got Ernie to keep quiet.

They stood, silently, staring at one another for nearly thirty seconds, before they started to hear voices again. A lag in the conversation and nothing more.

It meant Grace should still be alive. It meant whoever had her, likely Cuba, was going to talk her to death.

"You come. We rescue her," Ernie said. He waved his gun the way they needed to go, and Baker finally nodded.

It was the right thing to do. As much as he didn't trust Ernie and likely trusted Grace even less, Baker knew he couldn't walk out and head back home without at least trying to help.

What if Ernie and Grace both died today, because he didn't help them?

There really could be a treasure trove so close for the taking, and if he quit he'd never know.

"Fine. Let's go find the stairs and rescue the princess," Baker said.

FORTY-ONE

Rick had never wanted to get out of Mexico more in his life. They'd lived here for a long time, and he thought he and JoJo would continue to live out the rest of their lives here, whether in this town or another. But if the time with Cuba and treasure hunting had taught him anything, it was that nothing was permanent and life could be batshit crazy.

Looking at the AK-47 pointed at them by this raving lunatic with steroid muscles, Rick realized that they very well could be living their entire lives in Mexico. Very, very short lives.

"Did you have anything to do with this?" Rick whispered to Diego as the crazy man was on the phone.

"With what? This guy? Why would you think that?"

"I don't know, because you brought us into this wreck for some reason that I still don't know. Maybe you had him take JoJo to get leverage over me. Maybe Grace didn't escape, this guy took her also."

"And why would I do that? I don't need leverage over you. And if I wanted to do anything to any of you, I could have done it on my own property. You're thinking too much. Obviously, Cuba sent this guy."

Diego made sense, but with JoJo down in the basement and the things this guy was telling them he was going to do to her, Rick's capability of rational thought was short-circuiting. He needed to get to JoJo and then get them the hell out of here and out of the country. Anything and anyone who got in the way of that was a problem to be dealt with harshly.

Easy to say in my head rather than out loud to the guy with the automatic weapon in my face, Rick thought.

The problem was that he couldn't see a way out of this where the outcome wasn't decided by the man with the gun. He was hoping Diego would take the lead. He ran this section of the cartel. He should have some kind of negotiating skills. But Diego was just standing there, hands in the air, doing nothing.

Nacho was half-hidden behind Rick. He wondered if the man had noticed the kid. Maybe Nacho could sneak away and get help. But who was left to help them? The street rats weren't going to band together and take this guy down. Rick was also sure that the man in front of him would have no problem gunning down children.

"Good news for you," the man said after hanging up the phone. He pointed at Diego. "You get to be the last one to die. Bossman says he wants you with him. But you other two aren't leaving this house alive. And you, Rick. I think I'm going to make you watch what I do to your girlfriend."

He went on spewing a bunch of threats and violence, all of which Rick was positive he meant. Rick turned his eyes away from the man, hoping to tune him out. Hoping to have some miracle of an idea of escape pop into his head.

And it did.

Deliverance came not in a thought, but in his vision. His eyes landed on the busted and torched wall that led outside. Faces stared in at him. Faces he knew.

What hell was Ernie and Baker doing here? They must have somehow found out that Grace was in trouble and somehow figured out she was here. And Alberto? Where had he been in forever? Rick had almost forgotten the man existed.

It may have not been the best solution, or even a solution at all. What was Ernie going to do? The only thing the man attacked was a plate of food. And Baker, as far as Rick had seen of him, was basically dead weight. Alberto maybe had a chance at taking the guy out, but he would have to dodge a lot of bullets to do it.

Ernie put a finger to his lips and it took all his effort for Rick not to roll his eyes. But at least there was a chance now. Maybe if all three of them rushed the guy at once he'd only be able to kill two of them.

Instead of using the element of surprise, Ernie and Baker just walked into the room. The man spun and pointed the gun at Ernie, who was also locked in on him with his weapon. Baker stood there not sure what to do.

"Well, Ernie Patek. Baker Cioffi. Man, you all are making my job way too easy. All I need is the boat captain to show and that hot piece of ass from the cartel and I can just do you all in at once."

"Put the gun down. I have my men surrounding this place," Ernie said.

"I don't think so. Any men you had are with Cuba now. You're a lone wolf. Or maybe duck is the better word."

Ernie pulled the trigger, which shocked everyone. Especially Ernie. The bullet hit the man in the shoulder and embedded itself into the wall behind him. It gave Rick just enough time to tackle him to the ground and wrestle the weapon out of his hand. If the guy had use of both arms, Rick knew he wouldn't have had a chance.

He spun the gun around and smashed the butt into the man's face. Then again, since all the guy did was smile at him through a bloody mouth and broken teeth. By the fourth hit, he finally passed out. Rick, out of breath, leaned against the wall feeling like he was going to fall unconscious as well.

"Shoot him," Diego said to Ernie. "Never keep men like that alive."

Alberto came in and passed everyone and went into the basement. Rick followed, handing the gun off to Diego.

Halfway down the stairs a single shot rang out and by the time they made it back upstairs with JoJo and Grace, the man on the floor didn't appear to be breathing.

"Is he dead?" Baker asked.

"Of course he's dead. I shot him in the face," Diego said. "Are they ok?"

"We can speak for ourselves. And yes, we're ok considering the situation. What are you all doing here?" JoJo asked as Grace went to Ernie and gave him a hug.

Everyone started speaking at once, their words combining into some kind of new language that had never been heard before.

"Hold up, everyone. Shut up," Rick said, standing in the middle of them and holding his arms up. When it got quiet, he continued. "You, Diego. Why did you bring us here in the first place? You said something about Cuba not hurting us. Obviously you were wrong about that."

Diego shook his head. "Which one was his room?"

They led Diego to Cuba's old bedroom and he looked around, pulling out drawers, moving pictures. Finally, he grabbed an unopened Coke can and shook it, smiling. He twisted the bottom and it popped off and something small fell into his hand.

"Any captor worth his salt records everything," Diego said, holding up a mini-cassette. "I guarantee you there's enough on this to get the PFM on his ass. Stop him from leaving the country and put him in a cell so far underground he'd never be found again. You all want to be safe from him and get out of this? I bring this to my friend in the agency now. Before Cuba turns tail and leaves. This, my not-really-friends, is your get out of jail free card."

FORTY-TWO

When Maria returned to the villa, she was surprised to see Diego and everyone else were gone. They hadn't abandoned the property because the cartel men were still there.

They watched Maria but none of them spoke to her, letting her pass inside and not bothering her.

Maria knew she still had power. Some of these men had worked directly with her in the past, and they were either ashamed they'd betrayed her or they feared what she would do to them if she came into power again.

Diego has neutered me, but not for long, Maria thought.

Catalina had been silent the entire journey to the villa, and now she stared in wonder at the opulence surrounding her.

"This can all be yours and so much more, Catalina... if you do as I say." Maria didn't know if the girl was going to do what needed to be done or if she'd turn on Maria and try to do her own thing. The little girl was truly a wild card in all this, but it was a move Maria knew she had to make. It might be her only move, in fact.

Catalina ran her fingers over some of the statues in the hallway. She stopped and bowed low to the La Santa Muerte statue in the center of the great room as they entered it.

"I'll show you to your room. You'll wait there until I summon you," Maria said. "I need you to follow me first the plan, Catalina."

Catalina nodded, her eyes big in wonder as they moved from room to room. Maria took the long way upstairs, letting all of this sink in for Catalina.

The girl needed to see how her life could be if she followed directions. Follow the rules.

Maria smiled at the guards as she passed them, but none returned anything other than a slight head nod.

They know who is still in charge, Maria thought.

"Are you hungry? I can have the chef put together a spread of meats and tortillas for you. Maybe I'll join you for a quick meal on the balcony and we can watch for the approach of the others." Maria would need to make sure Diego didn't return before she knew he was back.

Things needed to be set into motion.

"I could eat. Mama said to never pass on a free meal." Catalina faintly smiled. "I miss her already."

Maybe you shouldn't have killed her then, you little monster, Maria thought. "Things happen beyond our control, Catalina. But guess what? I'm here for you. I will help guide you, and you will become a very rich girl who becomes an even richer, even more powerful woman someday. All you have to do is trust me. Can you do that?"

Catalina smiled and nodded her head.

"Excellent. Here is your room. It is one of the smaller ones but the rest are all taken," Maria said. She flung open the door dramatically and motioned for Catalina to enter first.

"This is my room?" Catalina asked, going inside and seeing the canopy bed, the expensive furniture, the huge mirror on the wall as well as a gorgeous view from the balcony.

"Yes, of course. For as long as you trust me, for as long as you do what needs to be done, this and so much more will be yours." Maria went to the balcony and waved her hand, Catalina at her side. "Isn't this view spectacular? We'll dine here. Look around your room and I will return with our food shortly."

"Thank you," Catalina mumbled, not looking at Maria. She was staring at the ocean, at the nearby town she used to live in in squalor.

This is the dream come true, Maria thought. She knew it was for her as a teenager, when Diego had gotten her pregnant and The Wolf in Colombia had taken her under his wing. The same as what she was doing for Catalina right now.

The Wolf. Maria smiled. Why hadn't she thought of him? "I'll be right back."

Maria rushed downstairs and found the cook, barking at him to make plenty of food for the little girl. Satisfied he was moving quickly, Maria stepped into the backyard near the pool.

A couple of guards glanced her way but made no move to intercept or chat with her.

They were all still wary of what she could still do, and she was going to find out herself with a phone call.

The Wolf answered on the third ring without saying a word.

"This is Maria. We need to talk," she said.

"Then talk. How are you doing, beautiful?"

Maria smiled. The old man always had a way with words. He was the head of the cartel, he'd killed countless men, women and children, he was ruthless in his business dealings, he was worth a large fortune, and he could cut you with a glare.

She also loved the old man, who had taught her so much. Taken her in like his own daughter, and taught Maria and Diego the ropes.

"I have a former lover who is doing things that you might not approve of," Maria said.

"Word has come back to me recently. Is there something he treasures?" The Wolf asked.

"Yes. And I have it. I am willing to share but not with him. He is a bad apple and he has tried to eliminate too many already. I need permission," Maria said.

"That is a big ask, especially with the player involved," The Wolf said. "I have sent a large group up there because word is another group wants his head and what he has."

"I have it, not him."

"I hope you are still a sharing type," The Wolf said.

"You have taught me well. I don't need any help on this, just a turn of the head with eyes that will see it," Maria said.

"You have an instrument?"

"I do. An unexpected one for him, too." Maria almost said Diego's name, which was a no-no on an open line.

"Then I trust you, beautiful. You have my support. For far too long things have been in motion that should be stopped, and I see a way for this to happen now," The Wolf said. "Thank you."

"I will see you soon."

The Wolf chuckled. "I hope you come bearing gifts."

"There will be many generous gifts with me. I assure you," Maria said and disconnected the call.

The food was almost ready and she told the chef to have it all delivered to the balcony upstairs, where the new girl was going to stay.

Maria joined Catalina back on the balcony. It looked like the girl hadn't moved an inch since Maria had left to make her phone call.

"From up here... they all seem so insignificant," Catalina said.

"Do you know why? Because they are. You have just figured out the first of many riddles in your life. This town is not the center of the universe. One day you will hopefully forget about it, too busy seeing the world, the real cities and the real people that can make you money. That can give you power and fame. This is not a life you want to lead in your old age," Maria said.

Catalina turned to Maria. "Then I will give up the treasure for these promises from you, ma'am."

FORTY-THREE

They decided being outside was the safer bet, despite the fact that they could be recognized. Once everyone was quiet inside the house, they couldn't help but hear the cracks and creaking of the walls and ceiling every time a breeze came through. The last standing part of the house would collapse at any time and they'd get buried under all the rubble. It was better to take their chances in the open.

Rick sat with JoJo across the street on the sand. He watched as the others gathered in small groups talking, or paced back and forth.

He liked Diego's idea of getting the recordings to some very bad men and having Cuba running for his life, but that would mean Diego would leave. As much as Rick didn't want him to be around, he seemed like the only person currently able to shield them from whatever was coming.

There was also a part of him that felt jealous at the idea that some faceless and nameless people were going to take Cuba down instead of him and the rest of them. From the look on Grace's face, it appeared that Rick wasn't the only one who wanted some personal revenge.

"Given up on me and going after the younger women now?" JoJo asked.

Rick put his arm around her. "Never. I thought you'd given up on me."

"I was close to it. Not gonna lie. But then I looked at Cuba, Alberto. Looked at Ernie and Baker. This Diego guy. I realized I didn't have it too bad with you. And if you do relapse, I'll just take your balls off. That should be enough to keep you on the right path. Heroin or balls? Your choice."

"I don't think Grace is happy to hand off Cuba to whoever Diego is planning on giving those recordings to. She looks upset."

"She's always pissed about something. I have to admit, it'd be nice to get the bastard back for everything he's put us through. But it would also be nice to get on a plane as soon as possible and to go Costa Rica, or Argentina, or fucking Antarctica. Anywhere but here."

"I'll do whatever you want. I just know we're not going to feel completely at ease until Cuba is permanently out of the picture. And I think the only way we'll know that for sure is for us to be the ones to confront him."

A rumbling came from up the street, out of sight. Before anybody had time to process it, a handful of Jeeps packed with men with guns drove by.

Has to be Cuba's men, Rick thought. *Why are they rushing into town?*

"It's time for us to move. Go our separate ways," Diego said. "Things are about to get crazy in town. I'll take care of Cuba.

You have my word." Diego lifted up the mini-cassette, as if any of them would have forgotten he had it.

"Do you think any of those men recognized us?" Ernie asked.

"No. Some of them would have stopped. These are all new guys. Cuba only had a couple left after they destroyed this house," Alberto said.

"It doesn't matter. They're going to get taken down when they find my men. I'd prefer I'm not also caught in the middle of it. I'd say it's nice to have known all of you, but we'd all know that's a lie. Get out of Mexico. Forget the treasure. That's the best advice I can give you."

Gunshots sounded in the distance as Diego walked away.

"Is he really just going to let us go like that?" Baker asked.

"He probably figures we have a decent chance at getting killed before we get out of this country," Grace said. "I don't think it matters to him one way or another. We're not a threat."

"So what do we do?" Rick asked.

"Get the hell out of here?" Baker looked uncomfortable as the gunshots increased.

"I'm not leaving until Cuba gets what's coming to him," Ernie said, attempting to hold the rifle in a threatening manner.

"Me too. I owe that jerk a lot of pain," Grace said.

"That's all fine and good," Rick said, carefully taking the gun from Ernie, "but I think we should at least get JoJo and Grace out of play. Alberto can take them out on the boat. Go somewhere until we're done with this business."

"Sexist much?" Grace put a hand on her hip and stared daggers into him. "I'm going to be there when he's on his knees begging to be let go. And we still have the treasure to think of."

"I don't think it's worth it at this point. JoJo told me about the girl and the other kids. If they have it, it's most likely hidden somewhere in town. And in case you haven't heard the couple million gunshots going off in that direction, it's not the safest place to be. We take Cuba out, then we say our goodbyes and go separate ways. Diego is damn well going to be going after the treasure and he's not going to be so easy going with us if he finds out we're still out there looking."

"We need more weapons," Baker said.

"What?"

"We need more weapons if we're going to confront Cuba. A guy like that isn't going to send everyone he has after the cartel and leave himself alone. He'll have security there. Enough that one gun isn't going to do anything to help us."

"We'll go back inside. Check the house," Rick said. "And I'm sure Nacho could find a way to get us …"

Rick looked around. For the first time, he realized that the kid was nowhere to be seen. He thought back to when they left the house and knew Nacho had come out with them. Diego didn't take him along when he left, so the kid disappeared sometime between then.

"Where is he?" JoJo asked.

"I saw him here a minute ago," Alberto said.

"Kid's like a magician. Too bad he's not older or I'd bring him on to work for me," Ernie said.

"We'll go after him," JoJo said, nodding at Grace. Rick thought he saw something unsaid pass between them. "You all deal with Cuba. Alberto, can you bring the boat to this beach?"

"I can get it close, but not enough for you all to board without some swimming involved."

"Do it. We find the kid, we probably find the treasure. Or at least get close to it. There's no harm in killing two birds with one stone." JoJo stood and walked over to Grace.

"Even if you find it, you can't transport it. The town is a nightmare right now, also," Rick said. A part of him wanted them to go after the treasure, but most of him was tense at the thought of JoJo going into a danger zone.

"We don't need all of it. Just enough to make our new lives a little more comfortable."

Everybody looked at each other, not saying anything, then one-by-one they nodded. JoJo looked at Rick. He took a breath and then nodded as well.

JoJo and Grace turned and headed down the road and around the curve. Alberto let out a breath.

"I guess I have to try to make it to the boat. I'll anchor right off there." He pointed to a spot next to an outcrop of land. "Should be deep enough there for the boat. Less time in the water for you guys."

Rick watched Alberto leave, then turned to Baker and Ernie. He checked the magazine and slammed it back into the gun.

"Let's go hunt us a piece of shit."

FORTY-FOUR

Maria and Catalina watched from across the street. When they saw Diego run off alone, Maria hesitated.

Should she reveal herself to the group and see if they'd help her to take down Diego and then Cuba?

Not likely. They seemed to be working with him now, and he simply walked away. They didn't have him as a prisoner and he wasn't their captor. Things have changed and there's no time to figure out who is working for who, Maria thought.

"Come, Catalina. We must follow Diego and see where he is going."

Catalina fell in line and the two females began shadowing Diego, who didn't have much of a lead and wasn't moving too quickly.

Maria knew it was because of the war happening in the streets all around them. Multiple gunshots. She thought she heard someone screaming in pain.

Cuba's men and the cartel men were officially at war. It didn't matter which side had pulled the trigger first. They would fight until only one side remained. Maybe both sides would be so depleted at the end it wouldn't matter who was the winner.

Maria worried she'd get caught in the crossfire. While The Wolf recognized her as a valuable part of the cartel still, she was sure Diego had told his men not to hold back if they saw her.

It would be easy for Diego to say he tried to warn her, tried to protect her, but there were too many bullets in the air and she was at the wrong place at the wrong time.

Maria was not going to lie when she told The Wolf and the cartel what Diego had been up to, and why she had killed him.

"Are you still with me?" Maria asked Catalina. The girl gave a faint smile and nodded, but Maria could see the girl's eyes were huge and at the sound of the next gunshot she jumped a bit.

"I don't think they're getting closer," Maria said. She still had Diego in sight up ahead and was happy he hadn't gotten into a vehicle and sped away.

Diego knew better. In a car you were an easy target, and speeding along you could be shot at from a hundred different angles and never know where your killer had fired from.

Like Maria, Diego knew these streets like the back of his hand. Catalina did, too. That might be helpful for what she had planned.

"We follow him until we can get him alone. Then we talk to him," Maria said to Catalina.

"I understand my part in this."

Maria stopped and smiled at the girl. "You have to trust me. This will be a very good thing for both of us. For all of us. You will never have to live in fear and you'll never have to look over your shoulder to see who is gaining on you. When you are with me you are under my protection and no one can touch you."

Catalina nodded but she was looking down the street at Diego. She pointed. "He's going into an alley."

"Then we follow," Maria said. She wasn't sure what Diego's destination was. There was only one way to find out.

When they got to the mouth of the alley, Maria put a hand out for Catalina to stay where she was.

Gunshots in the distance again, as if they'd all taken a siesta but were back to trying to kill one another.

Maria moved slowly and took a quick peek around the corner into the alley.

She pulled her head back just in time, as Diego fired and took out a chunk of building near her head. If Maria had been any slower she would've gotten concrete in her eye or a bullet in her cheek.

"Diego... I only want to talk," Maria said.

"Then show me your hands and walk out slowly."

Maria looked at Catalina and motioned for her to circle around. She turned back to the alley. "I would do that... but I don't trust you."

Diego laughed. "If I were in your shoes, I would not trust me, either."

"Now what? We can't yell like this. It will only draw attention, either from your men or Cuba's forces." Maria hoped Diego was not comfortable shouting this way and they could get closer to one another. She had a plan in her mind and a backup plan or two as well.

"I'll meet you in an hour at our spot," Diego said.

"No. We need to talk now." Maria didn't want him to rush off and do whatever he was trying to do, because it might make her life harder. What if he never showed up, too? Did it mean he was dead or he'd blown her off because he didn't need her, or even worse... what if he sent sicarios loyal to him to take her out?

When Diego didn't respond, Maria counted to five and stuck her head out again.

The alley was empty.

Groaning, she rushed down the alley to the other side, which emptied into a street usually busy with foot traffic.

There was no one outside right now except Catalina, who came around the corner.

"Did you see him?" Marias asked.

"No. There was a man with a gun but he didn't see me." Catalina ran up and got very close to Maria. "Is Diego gone then?"

Maria looked up and down the street but didn't see him. Where could he be going?

"Maybe we need to separate and find him," Catalina said.

Not a chance. I need to keep you in my sight at all times, little one. If you got the chance you'd stab me in the back in a heartbeat and think you were going to keep all of the treasure for yourself, Maria thought. "No. I think I know where he is headed. He's going to take this fight to Cuba."

Maria had no clue if this was really the case, but the idea had popped into her head in a panic when she was trying to think of a reason Catalina shouldn't be going off on her own.

"We stick together because that is the plan," Maria said. "Now we need to find out where Cuba is hiding before Diego does."

Has Cuba found a new villa to hole up in? Likely the men roaming the streets shooting at anyone who looked like a cartel member would know.

Maria decided she would take one of them down but not kill him. Not yet.

First, she needed information from the man and to find out where Cuba was.

Maybe I'll get lucky and find Cuba and Diego together and I can watch them kill each other, Maria thought.

"Let's go. Time to find an armed man and take him down," Maria said to Catalina, as if it was the easiest thing in the world to do.

FORTY-FIVE

Baker stayed in the back, letting Rick and Ernie move their way up the beach and through the small outcroppings of trees toward Cuba's hideout.

He imagined the three of them looked like idiots, walking fast and hunched over even though there was barely anything to hide their movements. The only thing that made him a bit less self-conscious was that there weren't any houses across the street where people might have looked out and laughed at them.

Ernie liked to tell him how people didn't take Baker seriously, but meanwhile they were making their way to Cuba looking like some kind of stupid buddy comedy movie.

"What are we just going to storm the place? You both realize we are three of the most unqualified people to lead an assault on anything but a Chinese buffet?"

"Shut up, Baker," Ernie said over his shoulder.

"Shut up, Baker. You're a loser, Baker. Nobody wants you on their dodgeball team, Baker. I'm tired of all you bullies giving me shit. I made something out of my life. I worked hard to get into the DEA."

"And look where it got you," Ernie said.

"None of this is my fault. You're the one who came down here and brought that maniac with you. You started the treasure craze. If it wasn't for you, I would have eventually gotten bored of tailing the cartel and went home long ago. Instead, everything you put into place conspired to keep me here."

"You can leave anytime you want. It would be the smart thing to do." Ernie tapped Rick on the shoulder, who stopped and turned to face them. "Look, I know you don't like it when I say this, but you really should try to get out of here. You've barely done enough to garner anyone's attention. Chances are, your name won't even get to the ears of anyone who might be looking for retribution. Go now and get yourself back home."

Baker shook his head. "I'm not useless. And I'm not leaving. Not now. We do this, then we head to the boat. Hopefully JoJo and Grace can get their hands on at least some of the treasure. Then we all drive away into the ocean. That's the plan. I'm not going home before we finish the plan."

"Can we keep moving?" Rick asked. "If you two want to argue out here, go ahead. But I'm getting to Cuba. And I also have the gun."

"I told you we'd need more weapons, but you just decided to charge full speed ahead," Ernie said.

"We don't need more weapons. I'm trained in this. Sure, it's been a couple decades, but old habits and all that."

Baker didn't comment on that. While initially he hadn't been sure, within a few days it came to him why Rick seemed so familiar. Ex-FBI. They'd worked on a couple of the same cases, though not physically together. Baker would do the research and information digging at his desk at the local DEA building and pass that on to the cross-agency team in the field. Rick had been a part of that.

He also knew that Rick not only wasn't FBI anymore, but was also on the wanted list for apparently leaking inside information and helping out with a shit-show of a heist attempt a while ago. He'd disappeared never to be heard from again.

Baker didn't care about any of that. While Rick had burnt out from a serious drug addiction, he was trained as a hot shot field agent, and he wasn't wrong that some of that muscle memory still remained. He'd rather have Rick holding the weapon than Ernie.

None of this meant he felt any easier about their situation as they crept closer to the house that just came into view.

There were two guards out front and two on the roof.

Same as at the last place, Baker thought.

"We can go in from the side," he said.

"What?" Rick asked as the three of them knelt behind a row of bushes.

"Cuba's a creature of habit. If this is anything like the other place, there will be one more guard out back watching the woods. Nobody will be outside at the side door. Worst case, there's a guard inside that we can take by surprise without making any noise."

They made their way further up the road in order to flank around and get between the front guards and the potential one in back. Baker wasn't worried about the men on the roof. That would just be timing.

They made it to the side door. Baker and Ernie were out of breath and Rick looked a little green in the face. Baker made a mental note to start a diet and exercise plan if he ever got out of Mexico. Then he crumbled up the note and threw it away. That was never going to happen.

A shadow moved in front of the stained glass on the door. Rick held a finger to his mouth and motioned for Ernie and Baker to back away. He rapped on the door and lifted the rifle so the butt was facing out.

The guard opened the door and stuck his head out. Whoever trained this guy needed to give back their training certificate.

Rick knocked him out on the first try and dragged him inside as Ernie and Baker followed him.

Baker took the man's sidearm.

"What are you going to do with that?" Ernie asked.

"Be useful." Baker racked a round into the chamber and felt a little like a bad-ass until two guards came around the corner and everybody froze for a second.

The three of them dove into a side room as the guards opened fire. So much for trying to be stealth.

Rick returned fire while Ernie crawled under the table and barricaded himself with chairs. Baker slid next to Rick.

"Still two?"

Rick nodded then pointed to the room across from them.

"You know how to work that handgun?" Rick asked. Baker nodded. "Cover me. I'm moving over there. Then we take these two out. I don't know how long it will take the others to get here, but there's no way they're not hearing this."

Rick ran across the hall into the other room as Baker opened fire on the two guards. His first shot got one in the head and another guard, who had come around the corner, got two in the gut. Baker looked at the gun in his hand as if to make sure it was really him holding it.

"Useless my ass," Baker grumbled at Ernie, who remained in his makeshift fort under the table.

Years behind the desk hadn't taken away his ability to hit a hostile target. All the joking and jabs and bullying at the agency had made him think he was everything he was being called.

Well, fuck those guys, Baker thought. *I am Dirty Harry. I am James Bond. I am the bringer of God's wrath.*

As he spun around the corner to return fire, he felt confidence and strength fill his body and mind. Then he felt the fire of a couple bullets hit him in the shoulder and hip.

I am... a moron, Baker thought as he dropped to the floor. Despite the pain, he didn't feel like he was mortally wounded. But he knew that his psyche would never recover from this.

FORTY-SIX

Diego watched as the three idiots somehow got into the villa. He was about to follow in their footsteps when he heard the shooting.

Maybe they'll all kill each other and make my life easier, he thought.

He glanced back over his shoulder, expecting Maria to appear at any moment. The woman would never let up and she was a decent tracker. She'd figure out where he was going.

Diego had done the legwork to find out where Cuba was now making his base, and it didn't take long to pay a couple of locals for the information.

It would mean leading Maria here as well, but that didn't matter. She would need to be dealt with at some point in the future. As soon as Diego had the treasure in his hand.

Diego hoped everyone showed up at this villa so they could all be managed. All be wiped out. Now he wished he'd taken a group of armed men with him, because no matter who Cuba hired, the sicario's could make quick work of them.

With all of the gunfire in the streets of the town, Diego was sure the cartel was getting the upper hand.

By the time he was done here everything should be back to normal.

All of his enemies would be dead and he'd be a very rich man.

Too bad Maria was not on the same page as me. We could be good together. Again, like the old days. We both came from the streets, from the dirt of this town, and we made something of ourselves. If she'd only gotten in line and saw what I was capable of, she could still live, Diego thought.

Diego crept closer to the villa and saw one of the guards trying to sneak in the way Ernie, Rick and Baker had gone.

"That would be too easy, sneaking up on them," Diego whispered and rushed across the lawn, hoping not to be seen.

The guard was hesitating, not fully committed to entering through the side door.

It allowed Diego to get to him quickly and slam the butt of his weapon against the man's head, knocking him to the ground.

"You'll be asleep for awhile," Diego said, taking the guard's weapon and extra ammo.

He glanced back over his shoulder, thinking he heard footsteps, but he couldn't see anyone.

Had there been more gunshots? Diego wasn't sure. He was focused on the task at hand.

No sense in rushing into the building and getting in the middle of a gunfight, either. He decided to fall back and see who came out of it alive. Better to be hiding nearby and watching, instead of moving room to room. Everyone inside wanted him dead.

And I want them all dead, Diego thought and smiled.

Sure no one else was in the immediate area, Diego crept back to the end of the property to find the perfect spot to watch. If anyone came out the front or the side door he needed to see them. If they came out the back door he hoped to be able to hear them.

There were several vehicles in the driveway and he had a good view of them, so anyone trying to drive out would be seen as well.

Diego had it all planned out. If anyone walked out of the villa he would shoot them. The hope was that the last man standing came out and was the last man dead.

With the additional weapon he had more than enough ammo.

There was no one on the roof anymore, which meant all of the guards had rushed inside to fight.

Diego almost felt sorry for Ernie, Rick and Baker, because none of them were real men. They were not fighters like he was, born and raised on the street.

Pampered Americans. He was betting they were already dead. He pictured the three of them entering through the door and immediately being surrounded by hired killers, who smiled as the three men cowered and begged for their lives. Wetting themselves in the process.

Diego knew if he'd walked into the building, even a few feet, he'd see their bodies. Smell their fear and the fact they'd shit themselves before they were even dead.

No movement from his position and he didn't hear anymore gunshots. Had there only been a few, as soon as the trio of idiots entered, or had he missed some?

Diego needed to find the treasure and wondered if letting everyone die was a good move. Maybe someone, anyone, knew where it was right now. Had it in their possession.

He realized if anyone had it they would have tried to leave Mexico already. Diego had every route accounted for, and if anyone tried to move even a few coins or whatever else the treasure was, he'd know about it.

The Wolf will be very pleased with me once I share the treasure with him, Diego thought.

Not that he was going to give it all over. Not even close. Maybe ten percent. The rest he would hide away and save it for later. Once time had passed and he was sure no one questioned him, he could slowly move piece by piece and get rich. Nice and slow.

Diego got comfortable and found a good spot on the ground to kneel. Weapon at the ready, he kept his head moving back and forth between the front and side doors.

No one was going to get past him.

"I wouldn't move if I were you, except to slowly lower your weapon," Maria said, stepping into his line of sight.

Diego was about to turn the weapon on Maria and hoped to catch her off guard, but then he felt the barrel jammed into the back of his head.

"Who–"

Maria shook her head. She had her own weapon in hand, aimed at Diego. "Never mind who is pressing the Glock into your skull. Eyes on me. If you make a move you will die. Very simple. Now... lower the damn gun."

Diego had no choice. Who was with Maria? There were a few options. One of the women. The boat captain. Maybe even Cuba himself.

"Now what do we do, Maria? It seems you are in charge. Tell me... do you have the treasure? Is there even treasure?" He put the weapon down on the ground but knew he still had his original weapon behind him.

Diego felt a hand at his back and the backup weapon was now gone, too.

Maria smiled. "Yes, there is a vast treasure. I've seen it, in fact. It is in my possession."

"Then we can work together to liquidate it. The Wolf will reward both of us for it," Diego said.

Maria shook her head. "I've spoken to The Wolf already. You have not, which makes my claim on it the legitimate one. It means that I am in control and it means that I decide your fate."

"You cannot kill me," Diego said. "The Wolf and the cartel would not allow it."

"No, you are correct." Maria lifted her gun to the sky but Diego still felt the barrel at the back of his head. "But I'm not going to kill you."

Diego needed to turn and see if he could get the gun away from whoever it was behind him, but knew Maria would shoot him. Not to kill but to wound.

And then whoever this was could finish Diego off.

Maria looked past Diego as she lowered her weapon again, aiming at his crotch. "Grab his gun and let him see who his killer will be."

When the little girl stepped out and took his other weapon, giving him a smile, Diego was impressed. "She's the same age as you, Maria. When you had your first kill."

"And she is about to get another kill. She has several already this week," Maria said and smiled.

FORTY-SEVEN

Cuba should have been packing, but instead he was laying on the bed, feet on the floor, with a glass of scotch resting on his chest. He couldn't remember the last time he went through a day without having a drink or twelve. The entire trip and wasted efforts finding the treasure had driven him to use booze to block out the crushing sense of failure.

He didn't think of himself as a failure. It was everybody around him. All the idiots he'd brought on to find the treasure who failed at their jobs. Hopefully Captain Jonah was almost done taking care of them all.

Technically, Cuba didn't need to have them killed, but he'd always had a policy of scorched earth when it came to the people he brought on for jobs. If it didn't work out, take everyone out and start with a clean slate.

He reached for the bottle of scotch on the nightstand and knocked it over. It fell, empty, onto the hardwood floor and shattered. Now he'd have to get up and walk all the way to the kitchen for another one.

I really should be getting ready and getting the hell out of here, Cuba thought.

Why would he rush, though? His men could hold off the cartel from coming up this way. And if they didn't defeat them in town, they would surely take enough of them out so that the remaining men at the house could pick off the stragglers. That is if they hadn't turned tail and ran back to Diego.

Cuba sat up and held his head as the room spun. He closed his eyes and waited for the movement to stop. He stood and walked to the en suite bathroom to pop a couple Tylenol. His head was pounding so much it felt like there was gunfight happening in his brain.

He stared at himself in the bathroom mirror before frowning.

Wait, those are bullets, he thought.

Cuba grabbed his Colt 1911 from the nightstand and opened the door to the bedroom. The sound of gunshots was immediately louder. They were coming from downstairs, far enough away to not be an immediate danger, but still too close for comfort.

Had the cartel men really made it here already?

One of his men ran up the steps and beelined toward him when he saw Cuba in the doorway.

"We must go, sir."

"What is going on?"

"Men. Three men on the inside. They're attacking and they're making progress. I don't think you'll be safe here much longer."

"Cartel?"

"I don't think so. Two fat men and a pale, junkie looking guy."

Welcome to my home Ernie, Baker, and Rick. Too bad you can't stay, Cuba thought.

"One of the fat men is shot, but they're still making their way here. Almost all of the guards are down. We must leave now."

Cuba walked to his dresser and opened the top drawer. He rummaged through the socks and underwear until his hand gripped the small remote he was looking for.

"Last I heard, the cartel in town is also taking down our men. They could be here any moment. Please, sir, it's time to evacuate."

Cuba was about to respond when his cell phone rang.

"Is the chopper ready?" Cuba asked.

"We've had to shut down, sir," the pilot said over the phone. "A group of armed men showed up. They look like cartel. I don't know how they found us."

The pilot continued to speak as Cuba disconnected the call and tossed the phone onto the bed.

"Sir?" the guard asked.

Cuba shot the man in the head and watched him drop to the ground.

"No way out. Cartel everywhere. Can't let them get a hold of me. No, definitely cannot," Cuba said, eyeing the pressure trigger remote that would set off all the explosives in the house that he had planned on detonating once he was far enough away. "At least take out Ernie and those assholes. End it on a high note. Wait for the cartel to flood the house. Then... boom."

Cuba glanced up, noticing the shooting had stopped. At the top of the stairs, Rick stood pointing a weapon at him. Ernie was panting next to him while Baker made it up the last couple stairs, trailing blood behind him. From the looks of him, he didn't have much blood left to lose.

"Come to say goodbye?" Cuba asked.

"You're not going anywhere," Rick said. "I just haven't decided whether to shoot you right now or hand you over to the cartel. Killing you might be letting you off too easy compared to what the cartel will do to you."

"You can't kill me, Rick. And I don't mean because you don't have the balls to do it. Although, I'm on the fence about that one." Cuba lifted his hand. "This is a pressure trigger. You kill me, my thumb comes off this trigger and the entire house goes up in a big fireball. You, me, Ernie, and Baker go up in flames. Judging by how Baker looks, that might not be the worst thing."

"And if I don't shoot you, the cartel will come anyway. You're screwed either way."

"Correct, Rick. The question is, are you three still screwed? Take me where you're going and I'll let all of us walk out right now. I can blow the place when the cartel walks inside from wherever I am. Then we part ways as if nothing happened."

"You want us dead. Tried to kill all of us. You'll just do the same thing once you're out of danger," Ernie said.

Cuba laughed. The booze was still running through him, but he felt it starting to wear off. He didn't blame the cartel for coming after him. That was their job. He knew how important it was to do your job in this line of work. These three, however, were to blame for everything. For his current situation with no way out. It would be much more satisfying to take them with him to whatever came after this life ended.

"You're right. Might as well just do it now."

Baker moved a lot faster than Cuba thought the big man could. Especially with a couple of bullet holes in him and emptying out like a busted water pipe.

Cuba felt a hand grip his, a thumb holding down his thumb. Then he hit the ground, Baker falling on top of him, and all the air rushed out of his body.

"Go now," Baker said to Rick and Ernie. "I have him but I'm not doing so well, so I don't know how much longer I can hold his finger on this trigger."

"Baker, we–" Ernie began to say.

"Don't be an idiot and start giving me a speech like in the movies. Just go."

Cuba, through tunnel vision, saw Rick grab Ernie and watched them run out of sight. He looked Baker in the eyes. He tried to struggle, but the man's body held him in place and his grip was like a vice. Men on the edge of dying seemed to find a strength buried deep down that they never knew was there.

A minute passed while Baker just stared at him.

"You can't hold me down forever, Baker. They've got to be out of the house by now. Let me go and I promise I won't blow the place up. I can help you out. We get out of here alive and you'll get whatever you want. And your wife will get the best care possible. It's your only choice. I mean, look at you. What do you even think you're doing right now?"

Baker's eyes hardened and Cuba knew it was over.

"Being useful, you piece of shit."

Cuba felt his thumb being pulled off the trigger and the world erupted around him before everything went black.

FORTY-EIGHT

Maria nodded at Catalina, who stepped forward and aimed the Glock at Diego's head.

"Do you remember that gun, Diego? You gave it to me. Showed me how to shoot it. Showed me how to kill a man the right way, by looking him in the eyes as you pulled the trigger."

Diego smiled. "And yet, here we are... with you making a child do your dirty work."

Maria shrugged. "I really had no choice. If I got my hands dirty, directly by pulling the trigger, The Wolf might not be so happy with me."

Diego stopped smiling. "The Wolf approved this? I don't think so."

"I guess you will never know. Did you really think you could hide the treasure and what you were doing?" Maria asked.

"We were doing this. All of us are guilty, and does it really even matter? The Wolf would get his cut in the end. He knows I was good for it," Diego said.

"Does he, though? You never mentioned it to him. I've stayed in constant contact with The Wolf and I'll be delivering his share of the treasure soon enough." Maria grinned and put a hand on Catalina's shoulder. "The boy, Ignacio, found it.

Catalina here stole it from him. Like I would've done to you when we were their age, right?"

Diego nodded. "I would've expected nothing less from you. There is no loyalty. What is the saying we always used?"

"There is no honor among thieves," Catalina said. "Can I kill him now?"

Maria and Diego both laughed.

"One less person means one less cut of the treasure," Maria said. "Before you go... I did at one time love you. Ignacio is my pride and joy, even if he came from a part of you."

Diego seemed to relax, as if he was accepting his fate. "We did have a good time while it lasted. Perhaps we'll see one another in the next life."

"Hopefully I'll find another person to shoot you in the head, too." Maria lifted her hand from Catalina's shoulder and the child pulled the trigger.

Diego was dead, his body falling to the side and resting in the grass.

"Now, Catalina, your last lesson," Maria said and placed her weapon against the girl's head.

"No, no." Catalina started to turn, leading with the Glock, but Maria shot her in the back of her head.

"I could never trust you. I know you'd try to kill me as soon as my back was turned. You are just like me at your age, which is why this had to happen. I'm sorry," Maria said. "You also screwed over Ignacio, my son. I cannot forgive you for that."

Maria turned back to the house and saw Ernie and Rick running in her direction.

She raised up her weapon and the house behind them exploded.

Maria fell to the ground and Ernie and Rick landed not too far from her.

"What just happened?" Maria stood, gathering the two weapons from the ground.

Ernie was huffing and puffing, but Rick cleared his throat and spoke. "Cuba had it all wired to blow. Finger on the trigger. Baker, the poor bastard, wrestled Cuba long enough we could escape."

Maria had the Glock ready to shoot both of these men, but instead she tucked it in her waistband. "I'm done with the killing. Where is my son? Where is Ignacio?"

Ernie and Rick both looked at one another.

"You lost my son?"

Rick put up his hands. "No, ma'am, we kept him out of harm's way. That's all."

"I will trade you a portion of the treasure for my son. How does that sound?" Maria asked.

Ernie frowned. "Why would you do that?"

"Because he is my son and it is the right thing to do, you idiot." Maria sighed. "If your daughter is still alive, now would be the time to make amends with her. She is a fighter. Grace is fierce. You need her on your side, Ernie Patek."

Rick chuckled.

"And JoJo is equally strong and the best thing that likely ever happened to you, Rick whatever your last name is. You need to get in line and stay the course," Maria said. She smiled. "I have the treasure." She glanced down at Catalina. "This little monster stole it from my son, and now I have it back."

"You could shoot both of us and take it all for yourself," Ernie said.

"Please don't give her ideas." Rick groaned.

"Wait until you see what it is, exactly. It fills a corner of a warehouse. More than we could ever hope to spend, more than one person will be able to carry," Maria said. She put up a finger. "But… there is a way to do this. The right way. Diego is no longer in charge. Obviously." Maria waved a hand at his dead body. "I am back in power, and I will call the local police to stop this stupid war that Cuba has started. He is dead and his men need to either leave the country or die."

"What way is there to do this?" Ernie asked.

Maria sighed. This man only cared about the treasure, only cared about himself.

"I want Grace to be safe. I want her to have my share, too. I've put her through so much. I will use my part of the treasure for her to have safe passage back to her home," Ernie said.

"You surprise me. No one will need to pay off anything, but the only way this will work is if the cartel gets a sizable portion of the treasure. Forty percent, in fact. I think The Wolf will be happy with that, and he will be able to liquidate the other sixty percent and the rest of us can divvy it up and go our separate ways." Maria put her hand out. "I give you my word."

Ernie and Rick shook her hand.

For a few minutes, the trio stared at what was left of the villa. Smoke rose up into the clear blue sky, and the smell of burning meat hung in the air. Many people had been killed in the explosion.

"I could go for some tacos," Ernie said. "And when we split the treasure, an equal share needs to go to Baker's widow. She is dying or something. It would be a nice gesture to help the woman and tell her what a hero her husband had been."

Maria smiled. "Again, you surprise me. I assumed you were selfish and arrogant and nothing more than a shallow man."

Ernie shrugged. "Maybe I am but I'm having a moment. An epiphany. I think we need to do the right thing, especially after all we've been through. The survivors deserve to be treated fairly and we put a lot of effort into getting this treasure... even though I guess in the end you got it."

"Ignacio got it." Maria looked at Rick. "What do you call my son?"

"Nacho. He hates it, so I will keep calling him Nacho until we part," Rick said.

"And when he is bad or he acts up I will call him Nacho to remind him of all of this." Maria heard the sirens and waved for Ernie and Rick to help her with the bodies. "We need to toss them into the fire before it goes out. We're wasting time."

"Won't the girl be missed?" Ernie asked.

"No. She killed her mother. She killed all of the street urchins. She was a nasty little girl," Maria said.

She reminded Maria of herself at that age, and knew she hadn't come far enough after all these years. She needed to do better for not only her family, not only the cartel, but for everyone she encountered that wasn't an enemy.

FORTY-NINE

Alberto sat, leaning back, on his boat as it swayed with the swells. Night was coming on when he anchored just offshore of Cuba's old house. The gunshots started shortly afterward.

He shook his head, oddly calm considering they were all about to make a run for it. That was, if Rick, Ernie, and Baker survived their assault and if Grace and JoJo made it in and out of town in one piece.

Alberto didn't know why they couldn't all just meet him at the dock. He guessed this was probably the best. In case they were being followed or chased, they would have a better chance getting here than all the way to the boatyard.

It was about a fifty-foot swim from the end of the outcropping to the boat. It was as close as he could get without risking damage, whether from bottoming out or being tossed around. The water was a bit more feisty than he had thought. Swimming to the boat meant they would have to time their jumps for when the tide went out, otherwise they risked being slammed back against the rocks.

Good thing I stole that dinghy, Alberto thought.

He'd been about to leave the dock and head to his current position when it occurred to him that things would go much smoother with a separate boat to bring them across the water. And he knew plenty of boat owners in the dock who never locked down their dinghies. It was a no brainer.

It was one of those pain-in-the-ass blow-up ones, but luckily Alberto had an air machine on board. His lungs wouldn't have been able to handle that.

He was thinking about how the logistics of getting everyone on the boat would work when a bright light, then a fireball lit up the sky. The sound of the explosion came about a second later and shook the boat. The water around him vibrated as if a million little pebbles had been dropped into the ocean.

He watched as the fireball went from bright to a dark gray cloud that began to drift inland, pushed along by the ocean breeze.

Alberto was at a loss. Did everyone die in that explosion? Could anyone have survived? It definitely wasn't Rick or the other two who set that off. They only had one gun among them, let alone however much explosives were used to make that cloud.

He guessed he wouldn't know until he either saw them running up the beach, or it was time to leave with whoever had made it back alive. Either way, it was time to get things in motion.

Alberto dropped the dinghy overboard, its line tied tight to the boat clamps. He attached the ladder and carefully lowered himself onto the dinghy. The swells were increasing in size and frequency.

Whoever wants to leave better get their ass down here quick, Alberto thought.

He got the small motor started and made his way to the outcropping. Coming in was tricky, but he managed it. He would have preferred not to have smashed his knee on a rock, but it was better than bashing his head in them.

After he tied the boat, he waited, watching the beach for any figures moving in.

The dinghy was big enough to hold three people. That would mean three trips. Hopefully nobody was after any of them.

Two people came from around the corner and headed toward him. He immediately recognized Ernie's weird way of running. They came up and stopped, breathing hard.

"No time to dilly-dally. Let's go," Alberto said. "Baker?"

Rick shook his head and got in the boat.

By the time Alberto got them offloaded, JoJo and Grace were waiting for him.

"Where's the kid?" Alberto asked.

"Safe," was all JoJo said.

They got situated on the boat and Alberto scanned the beach.

"Nobody coming after any of you? That's a little hard to believe."

"Things turned out a little different than we thought. Are you ready to be rich? Or, at least, very comfortable financially?" Rick asked.

"What are you talking about?"

Rick explained the situation with Maria and what she proposed. JoJo jumped in when she needed to add something from their end of the story. Apparently they had run into Maria and Nacho in town and were let go without any issue and offered the same stakes Maria gave to the guys.

"And you trust her? She's just going to make sure we all get our fair share and we wipe our hands of all of this?" Alberto asked.

"No, I'll never trust her with anything. But that doesn't mean she won't follow through. We'll find out. Either way, whether she does what she said she was going to do or not, we all need to get the hell out of here."

They pulled the dinghy in and Alberto started the boat.

"So, how is she going to find us if we're all leaving and splitting ways?" Ernie asked.

"She'll find us. I don't doubt that. She's too clever to lose track of us," Grace said.

"Doesn't make me feel any better. I don't need eyes on me for the rest of my life. Kind of defeats the purpose of disappearing," Alberto said.

"We're too boring for her to actually expend energy on. She'll just know where we are, and if she keeps her word, we'll all be in for a surprise unboxing soon. For now, let's get the hell out of here." Rick leaned back as the boat moved away from the beach.

Alberto took them all out, far out. He went far enough that the land was just a foggy glow in the distance. Far out enough that the boat would look like just another white cap on the water. He hoped the swells would pick up, that the sea would get angry and help camouflage the boat and the direction they were headed in.

They all agreed to dock in on one of the tourist traps a little farther north, say their goodbyes, and go their separate ways.

Alberto felt kind of sad. None of these people were his friends, but they'd all been in a unique enough situation that a bond was formed. He would allow himself to worry about them for just a little while, then he would continue on with life under no expectation they would ever see each other again.

If we are all smart, we'll make sure this is our last gathering, Alberto thought.

"Rick. In the cooler."

Rick pulled out a bottle of tequila and laughed. They each took a swig off the bottle and Alberto poured some into the ocean as a bribe to allow safe passage.

Then, he turned the boat into a particularly dense fog patch and they were enveloped by the cloud, swallowed into whatever their lives would be.

FIFTY

Her name was now Julie and he was Robert. They'd spent the last three weeks in a mountain villa overlooking Palermo. Before that they'd been in Brazil and before that Finland.

"Where should we visit next?" She smiled and tossed a grape into her mouth, reaching for her wine glass.

Robert put a hand on her hand and squeezed it. "Wherever you want to go, JoJo... er, Julie." He sighed. "Can't we use our real names?"

She shook her head. "If we turn up anywhere in the world with our real names, we'll have several problems. You know the score and what we need to do. Have the past several months been bad at all?"

"No, I have to admit... this is the life," he said. "Can I be honest with you, though? I'm getting sick of lobster. I never thought I'd say that."

"So am I. God, I could go for a Nathan's hot dog on the boardwalk or a slice of New Jersey pizza," she said. They'd been eating fancy meals since they'd fled Mexico with their new identities.

And a lot of money in several offshore bank accounts.

Millions of dollars. Money they'd never be able to spend fully, and they'd invested a lot of it and therefore were making more money.

They'd decided to skim the profits off of the top and live a good life. Nice and simple.

"I wonder how everyone else is doing," Robert said. "I know you've been checking, too."

Julie smiled. "I have. They all seem to be doing well. Ernie made good on his promise and gave Grace his share of the treasure. For her part, she gave it back and they have also been traveling. As far as I can see, Ernie hasn't tried to find more treasure or done anything stupid."

"He'll get there soon enough, if we know Patek."

Julie chuckled. "True. Maria has been put in charge of Mexico for the cartel and made side deals with rival cartels so there are no wars. No killings. Just good business. Not that the cartel needs to play nice, since I'm told The Wolf was quite happy with the treasure given to him and gladly liquidated the rest for us."

"Alberto is where?" Robert asked.

Julie started to laugh. "He owns a fleet of fishing vessels in San Diego. He pretty much bought out anyone and everyone and hired all of the captains for his boats. I'm sure he is doing well."

"Baker's wife was taken care of, I presume?"

"Of course. In fact, Maria herself took care of it. Made sure she had the best doctors and twenty-four/seven support. The woman is in recovery and she was told what a hero her husband had been in Mexico. Since the DEA has washed their hands of Baker Cioffi, the cartel has been giving her money for her living expenses. Of course, she has no idea where the money is coming from, only that Baker did a favor for some wealthy individuals while in Mexico and this is how they repay his work and generosity."

Robert waved at the waiter and asked for another bottle of wine.

"Are we celebrating?" Julie asked.

"Yes, we are. I haven't asked you about anyone for several weeks. I wanted to distance ourselves from them but get a final tally on what they were doing with the money from the treasure. They all seem to be doing well." Robert frowned. "And what about Nacho?"

"His mother was given a villa just outside of town. Armed guards and is a known relative of Maria, who is highly ranked in the cartel. No one will mess with them. And yet..." Julie shrugged. "Ignacio is still running the streets. He formed a new crew and does what he does best. Hopefully as he gets older he won't get sucked into the cartel life. There are millions of dollars in bank accounts, collecting interest, for when he turns eighteen."

"Then all is well that ends well," Robert said.

"Except for all the people that were killed."

Robert waved his hand. "Yes, yes, I get it. I'm not making light of death. But we came out the other side and we're doing quite well. Do you love me?"

"Of course I do, although you drive me insane at times," Julie said.

Robert slid out of his chair and went down on one knee. "I had one piece of jewelry put aside from the original treasure, a ring that fits your style. I notice things and had it sized for you. JoJo, will you marry me?"

"Yes, but aren't we already married?"

"Legally I don't think so. I want a big wedding before we leave Italy. Whatever you want," Robert said.

"I want you to call me Julie."

Robert shook his head. "Sorry. I just... JoJo and Rick sound much better, don't you think?"

"Maybe we can change them again, down the line. After a few years. Once we're sure the United States government isn't looking for us, and whoever else wants us dead."

Robert put the ring on her finger and she held it up and smiled.

A few couples at other tables began to clap for them.

Robert had made sure no one was ever seated anywhere close to them, so they could talk and be normal together. Now he wished the tables surrounding them were filled with happy couples so they could get a good look at the ring and congratulate them properly.

After dinner they took a walk by the canal, hand in hand. They'd had two bodyguards with them at all times and one was ahead of them and one behind, very discreet and very deadly.

Robert and Julie worried word might get out how rich they were, and an added bonus of more people after them would happen.

They stopped near the railing and looked out to the water, the city lights reflecting off of it and creating a dazzling display.

Robert leaned over and kissed Julie. He was happy. He was grateful for her. Most importantly, he was clean.

No drugs for a long time and he had been slowly pushing the urges further and further away.

Ironically, he had so much money he could literally kill himself buying so much heroin or cocaine, but he wouldn't do that to JoJo. Sorry, Julie.

They walked back to their car and Robert held the door for Julie. He got a smile and another kiss for that gentlemanly move.

As he strolled around the car a couple of vehicles passed by and a man driving a red Fiat Panda caught his eye.

The driver glanced at Robert and Robert swore the man smiled.

"No. It can't be," Robert pointed before rushing to get into his own car. "It can't be."

"What's the matter?" Julie asked.

"I saw… someone from our past. But he's dead, right? Johnny Bell is dead." Robert was shaking his head.

"Yes, of course. His son told us that years ago. Why would he be in Italy? He doesn't strike me as someone who wants to travel and sightsee." Julie put a hand on Robert's arm. "You're getting paranoid. Maybe we will spend the next few days at home and not go out so much."

Robert nodded his head. "Yes, that might be the right move. I'm tired, that's all. Maybe I had more wine than I thought."

"I'll drive. I'm fine." Julie got out and walked around the car, opening Robert's door.

Robert got out and walked to the passenger door, staring into traffic at all of the cars driving by.

No way it was Johnny Bell. He's dead. He'd never be in Italy. My mind is playing tricks on me, Rober thought.

Johnny Bell had been a bank robber. A man that had led a crew and not a very good one. Rick and JoJo had met working with Bell, and in the end they'd managed to escape to Mexico before they were arrested or killed.

Most of the crew had been arrested or killed.

Johnny Bell had definitely been killed. Rick-Robert knew it.

Then why did I just see him? This is insane. I need to relax, Robert thought and got into the car.

"How about Canada next?" Julie asked as she slid the car into traffic, the bodyguards right behind them in their vehicle.

"Canada? What's there to see there?"

"Moose. Hockey. Snow. A quiet cabin in the middle of nowhere. We could lie naked in front of a fire all day," Julie said.

Robert smiled. He liked the sound of that.

ABOUT THE AUTHOR

Armand Rosamilia is a New Jersey boy currently living in sunny Florida, where he write when he's not sleeping. He's happily married to a woman who helps his career and is supportive, which is all he ever wanted in life…

He's written over 200 stories that are currently available, including crime thrillers, supernatural thrillers, horror, zombies, contemporary fiction, nonfiction and more. His goal is to write a good story and not worry about genre labels.

He also loves to talk in third person … because he's really that cool.

ABOUT THE AUTHOR

Born the same week Animal House was released, Tom Duffy has been on Double Secret Probation ever since. ABBA was also on the top 10 music charts, and Andy Gibb was Shadow Dancing at #1. The author has no problem with any of these things.

Printed in Great Britain
by Amazon